THE DARK HOUSE
OF THE SEA WITCH

THE DARK HOUSE
OF THE SEA WITCH
BY JOAN G. ROBINSON

COWARD, McCANN & GEOGHEGAN, INC.

NEW YORK

Copyright © 1979 by Joan G. Robinson
First American edition 1979
All rights reserved. This book, or parts thereof,
may not be reproduced in any form without permission
in writing from the publishers.
First published in Great Britain under the title Meg and Maxie.
Library of Congress Cataloging in Publication Data
Robinson, Joan G
The dark house of the sea witch.
SUMMARY: On their own while their parents and house-
keeper are away, Meg and her brother make the acquaintance
of a neighbor they suspect is a witch.
[1. Brothers and sisters — Fiction] I. Title.
PZ7.R5664Dar   [Fic]   79-10845 ISBN 0-698-20494-8
PRINTED IN THE UNITED STATES OF AMERICA

Contents

1

Meg Waits to be Told

"You'll be all right with Hannah," said the children's mother. "We'll only be away one night."

Meg sat up. This was what she had been waiting to hear, wondering when they were going to be told.

The Bennett family—father, mother, Meg and Maxie—were on holiday at the same cottage they came to every year. With them was Hannah, the au pair girl, who had come to help. It was breakfast time, and they were waiting for Hannah to come back with the eggs from the farm.

"It's much more sensible for me to go up with Daddy," Mrs Bennett went on. "Saves the train fare, and we can drive up together. Then after Daddy's interview we can go to see Granny Bennett. She hasn't been very well."

Meg was silent. There was another reason, she knew. She waited for her mother to go on.

"I'll leave plenty of food so Hannah won't need to go shopping. There'll be nothing to worry about. You're quite old enough now."

Meg shook her shoulders impatiently. Of course she was. But what had that to do with it? You could be worried about all sorts of things even if you were a hundred. Especially if your parents would never say outright what they were thinking. Not in front of the children, that was.

"So there's nothing to worry about," her mother said again.

The slight sense of dread in the pit of Meg's stomach gave a lurch. Whenever her mother said there was nothing to worry about, it always made her feel there might be.

"But why are *you* going?" she asked, staring at the pattern on her plate.

"Various reasons." Mrs Bennett got up from the table to put more bread under the grill. "There are one or two things to buy. You need new pyjamas, for one thing"—her back was turned—"and one or two things to fetch from home. Fancy our coming away and forgetting Maxie's wellies! I don't know how we could have forgotten them. I suppose I thought Hannah'd put them in."

"But you said you had an appointment," said Meg, tired of waiting to be told.

Her mother turned quickly with a bright interested smile.

"Did I, darling? When was that?"

"Yesterday. You told Daddy when he was shaving. You said you had an appointment with Dr. Miller on Thursday."

"Oh yes, just for a check-up! That's nothing to worry about. But Maxie really must have his wellies. I don't know what he'd do if it went *on* raining, with all this mud in the fields, though it is looking a little brighter."

"What's a check-up?" asked Meg, steadily persistent.

Mr Bennett put down his newspaper. "Just to make sure she's all right. That's all, Meg."

"Isn't Mummy all right?"

"Yes, of course she is."

"Then why is she going to see Dr. Miller?"

"Darling, darling," said Mrs Bennett, coming back to the table. "I do wish you wouldn't go on at things so. Like a dog with a bone. There's nothing wrong with going for a check-up, and there's nothing wrong with me. I know I wasn't very well a few weeks ago. I even had two days in bed—and I should think it's the first time you've ever seen that happen! But I haven't seen the doctor since, so I thought I might as well pop in at the same time as seeing to all the other things. Just to make sure I'm all right, which I'm sure I am. Satisfied now?"

Meg nodded. She supposed she was. But it was annoying this feeling that she had to *drag* information out of them. Why did they always think you didn't know about things? You couldn't help knowing—not unless you were like Maxie. Maxie didn't need to know things. He just took them as they came, knowing people would make a fuss of him whatever happened. But she was the oldest, and she needed to know what was happening, and what was going to happen. She had always felt like that.

It was easy for Maxie. People had always made a fuss of him. Partly because he was beautiful. Partly, Meg felt, because he was a bit barmy. If he was not actually barmy, that was the impression he gave you, staring with those great wide eyes as if he was listening to nothing all the time. 'A fairy child' Granny had called him once. What a thing to call a boy! Even now, breaking up his toast into little boats to float in his milk, he was looking so delicately absorbed that no one would think of scolding him for making a mess.

Hannah had come in with the eggs. She had picked out the best brown speckly one specially for Maxie. Meg had known she would, but she bore her no grudge for it. It was only to be expected. All the same, if there had been a chance Meg would have liked to suggest to Maxie that the egg might be bad. Or that there would be a live chicken inside it that would peck him fiercely when he broke the shell, a chicken that would grow larger and larger until it became a fierce dragon, threatening to gobble him up.

She was often beastly to Maxie like this. She did not want to be, but she could not help it. She felt guilty about it sometimes. And that was a worry.

There must have been a time, she felt, long, long ago, when everything had been nice and cosy, going on and on the same with nothing to worry about. It would have been before Maxie was born, she supposed. She could not really remember it, but she wished it was like that now.

This morning, though, things were looking brighter. It had stopped raining. And the trip to London had been talked about. That was a relief. It was one thing knowing about something, and another thing actually being told. She turned to her mother.

"What colour new pyjamas?" she asked.

"Oh, I don't know, darling. What colour would you like? I'll have to see what they've got."

Mrs Bennett turned her attention to Hannah. "I've

just been telling the children—" and she began explaining about the trip to London all over again.

Hannah listened earnestly, nodding her head and repeating the last words of every sentence as if she were having a lesson—which Meg supposed she was in a way, since Hannah had told her soon after she came, "I only come to learn the English. I am stoodent."

Watching her mother now, waving her hands about as she talked, Meg felt sorry for Hannah. It must be horrid, she thought, being so far away from home, and only knowing what was happening there when you got a letter. And being talked to in that special voice, loud, with a rounded mouth, which her mother seemed to think helped understanding. Poor Hannah, she was nice, even if she did seem like half a person because she could only speak half the language, which wasn't fair on her . . .

"So we will only be away one night, Hannah," Mrs Bennett was saying, brightly smiling.

"One night?" Hannah repeated.

"And a day, of course. A day and a half to be exact." There was no answering smile from Hannah. "You do understand?" Mrs Bennett's smile grew anxious.

"I understand."

"And I'm sure you'll manage very well."

Hannah looked glum. "I go upstairs now to make bed. Please excuse," she said, and left the room.

"What *is* the matter with her?" said Mrs Bennett, once Hannah's footsteps could be heard clumping about overhead. "Do you know, Meg? Doesn't she like it here, or what?"

Meg considered. "I think she does, quite. But she doesn't like cows."

"But we don't keep cows, for goodness sake!"

"No, but I suppose she might meet some. We nearly did yesterday. That's how I know."

"And d'you mean to say she's going around with that worried gloomy face just because she might meet some cows?"

"Oh no, she's *worried* because she hasn't had a letter from home. She says her mother writes every week, and she hasn't had one since we came."

"Then what on earth are we talking about cows for? Poor girl. But we've barely been here a week. It'll take an extra few days for letters to be sent on. I must tell her."

Sitting on the doorstep after breakfast, Meg was sorting through a heap of last year's shells when she heard her parents' voices through the kitchen window.

"I wish there was some way they could get in touch," her mother was saying. "Just in *case* they needed to."

"They won't need to," said her father. "But isn't anyone on the phone round here?"

"Only Mrs Jarvis."

"Oh lord." Meg heard her father grunt. "Well, I suppose in an emergency Hannah could go. But don't worry, there won't be an emergency."

"No, I suppose not." Mrs Bennett heaved a great sigh. "All the same I do wish Mrs Jarvis would move, and let some *ordinary* family come and live there."

Meg held her breath to listen. Anything about Mrs Jarvis held a creepy fascination for her. Partly because she was always talked about in that mysterious, guarded voice that children are supposed not to be able to hear. She had not heard much, it was true, but enough to know that she lived alone and had no visitors, that sometimes there were lights on in her house all night, and she forgot to pay her bills. She put down the shells she had been holding, and moved closer to the window.

"It could be mostly hearsay," her father was saying. "Being isolated the way she is, and living alone all the year round in that creepy place, would be enough to make anyone . . ."

Make anyone what, Meg wondered?

"Yes," said her mother, "but Mrs Pacey at the paper shop—she always calls her 'that sea-witch woman,' goodness knows why. Perhaps because she goes beachcombing . . . she told me . . ." Meg could only hear snatches of sentences now. Her mother's voice had dropped to a mere murmur. ". . . all the lights on . . . shouting in the fields and nobody there. I tell you, it's spooky."

She heard her father laugh. "Oh yes, I heard all about that in the pub! There's no holding them once they start. There'll be a spurious ghost there next. You see if there isn't! I wonder now—" and he seemed to be thinking—"Look, Judy, why don't we ask her round here some time? She's our nearest neighbour, after all. It seems unfair to judge her without knowing her."

"Not with the children!" Mrs Bennett sounded dismayed.

"No, of course not. After they're in bed, I meant."

A plane flew overhead and Meg could hear no more.

She went round to the front of the cottage. Maxie was squatting on the grass, with his new kite laid out in front of him. He jumped up when he saw her and, holding the kite behind him, backed slowly away. It annoyed her to see him looking so suspicious and silly.

"Don't be stupid, I don't want that thing," she said. He looked unconvinced, and this annoyed her still more. She moved closer, her eyes wide and dark. "But I'll tell you something." He backed away, staring into her eyes. "*She's* coming," she said softly. It was not the first time she had used Mrs Jarvis to frighten him. She dropped her voice to a whisper. "*She's* coming. She's coming here!"

His mouth fell open. "Who?"

"You know. Mrs Jarvis. They're going to invite her."

Maxie stared. "I don't believe it," he said. Then he picked up his kite and ran full tilt round to the back of the house.

2

The Private Road

"I have still no letter," said Hannah, plodding along the track towards the village that afternoon.

"Never mind," said Meg, "I expect it will come soon. Mummy says it will. Tell us some more about your brother and the wedding."

Hannah brightened, as Meg had known she would, and launched once more into the story of her brother and his girl friend who were soon to be married.

It was hard listening because Hannah kept getting stuck for words, and Meg, who had lost the point of the story quite soon, could only make wild guesses as to what the words might be. But she had already gathered from previous talks that Hannah's brother was handsome, Heidi was beautiful, and everyone at home was looking forward to their wedding in October. Also that Hannah would be wearing pink. "Like this—so," she had said a few nights earlier, pointing at the soap in the bath rack. "Mein hat also," and Maxie had relapsed into foolish giggles at the thought of Hannah wearing a cake of soap on her head at her brother's wedding.

Today, as far as Meg could discover, Hannah was recounting a list of the wedding presents they were expecting. (How otherwise should there be a feather bed, twenty silver teaspoons, and a large frying pan involved—especially as the wedding was being held in church?) Whatever it was, it was boring. But it was nice for Hannah, Mrs Bennett had said, to have the children walk with her to the shops, so here they were.

The shopping done, Hannah stopped outside the post office.

"I shall go to ask one more time," she said, suddenly hopeful. "Perhaps my letter now has arrived. You can go on to home," and smiling and waving, she disappeared inside.

Meg looked at Maxie. "Run," she said.

"Why?" said Maxie.

"It's good for you," said Meg, not wanting to say aloud that she had had enough of the wedding. Obediently, Maxie ran. "No, this way," called Meg.

"Why?" said Maxie again.

"Because it's the best way."

What she meant was that if he went that way he would have to pass *her* lane. Even she found the idea a little frightening now. It was silly of him; he must know he might run into Mrs Jarvis. Perhaps he was just showing off. But he was still running on.

She hurried after him, and turning the corner into the coast road, saw him ahead. He was just passing the last of the cottages. After that it was nothing but high hedges all the way until he came to the turning with the notice which said 'Private Road.' It was here—if she was there—that Mrs Jarvis would be, at the corner of the muddy track that led to Rook Hall.

They had seen her there before, quite often. She had been sitting on the grassy bank with a basket, picking and eating blackberries, or gathering elderberries—to make wine, people said. At other times she had been standing there, staring, as if she were seeing the view across the fields for the first time, and was surprised by it. They had always hurried past, but knew when they turned their heads to look back, she would be staring after them.

Mrs Jarvis was tall and dark. She wore strange clothes, long raggedy skirts made of patchwork, that trailed in the mud, sometimes a sack over her shoulders, and huge, man-sized wellington boots. She was unlike anyone Meg had ever seen. Her hair was black with white streaks, and terribly untidy. But her eyebrows were pencilled heavily black, and there were round red patches on her cheeks as if she had made up her face in the dark in a terrible hurry.

Supposing she should turn out to be a witch after all!

Meg thought how often she had told Maxie she was, to frighten him, only half believing it herself; half believing it because there *was* something frightening about Mrs Jarvis. It was the way she had of staring at them—particularly Maxie—not smiling or saying hallo, just looking and looking, as if she had never seen a little boy before.

"Maxie!" she called. "Come back!"

But he was deliberately running away from her. Did it mean he didn't believe her any more? It had always been so easy to frighten him before. She had only to whisper to him "Run, Maxie, run! She's a witch and she'll get you if you don't look out!" and he would run, panting along beside her until they were both out of breath. And both frightened, in a way. It was funny how often Meg had managed to frighten herself as well, without meaning to. But she had not really believed it then, not seriously.

Now it was different. She ran faster, caught him up, and grabbed him by the arm.

"Maxie, don't be so silly! Not that way, unless you *want* to be caught. You know she's often there, at the end of her little lane."

"I don't mind," he said. "If they're going to invite her, it must be all right."

"*After we're in bed*, they said. We'd be safe upstairs then. You don't suppose they'd ask a witch with us there, do you?"

Maxie made a sudden dive and broke loose. He had run some way up the road when he called back: "Anyway I don't believe she is a witch!"

"Wait, Maxie! Wait! I'll tell you something—how I know."

But already he was rounding the bend.

When she turned the corner and could see the road ahead, she saw that he was wandering along quite unconcerned. He had probably forgotten about her. Certainly he was not worried about witches. He was weaving along the grass verge, peering now and then into the hedge, looking for old birds' nests. He was quite unaware that not three yards from him, partly hidden by a bramble bush, a gaunt figure was standing, still as a statue, waiting. It was Mrs Jarvis.

And she was staring, just staring, at Maxie.

Meg had no time to think. "Maxie, come back!" she called. "We're going the other way." Her voice sounded very unnatural but he did not seem to notice.

"No, I want to go this way," he said, not even looking up.

"Maxie, come *here*! There's something I want to tell you!" She ran towards him and, at the same moment, Maxie caught sight of two large boots in the long grass under the bush. It had just dawned on him whose they must be. He turned with a gasp and almost fell into Meg's arms.

She clung to him, seeing over his head Mrs Jarvis still standing there, unmoving, laughing silently. She felt frozen to the ground. That silent laughter was unnerving, sinister. If Mrs Jarvis had made a sound it would have been less frightening. A gold stopping in one of her teeth glinted. Her bright-dark eyes glistened as she turned them slowly from Maxie to Meg. Then, in a deep husky voice, she asked:

"Why don't you let him choose the way? Everyone must have a choice some time."

Not until Mrs Jarvis spoke was Meg able to move. Then she seized Maxie's hand, and dashed up the road with him, not stopping to look back until they reached the next bend. Mrs Jarvis was still there, standing in the same place, quite still, like a stone statue that had been out in all weathers, battered by the winds.

They ran on. They were half way home before they stopped for breath.

"I *told* you! You should have come when I called," said Meg.

"But how d'you know she's really a witch?" Maxie asked thickly.

"Because I do. I believe everybody knows it except us. That's why she lives alone. She's isolated, that shows you—like when you had that rash and everyone thought it was infectious—so other people don't catch it." Maxie nodded. He looked impressed. "Daddy said she was isolated," said Meg, repeating the important word. "And I bet you that's why there's that notice saying Private Road."

"My mouth's gone gluggy," said Maxie. "Did I get that off her?"

"No, I expect that was having to run so fast. But I'll tell you something else. There's going to be a spurious ghost there next."

"Where?"

"At Rook Hall, silly."

"What's spurious?"

"Spooky and furious, I should think, I'm not sure. Anyway that's what he called it, and Mummy said it was spooky, and she wished Mrs Jarvis didn't live here." She leaned forward, looking solemnly into his eyes. "But we're not supposed to know, so you'd better not say anything."

"All right, Meg."

Hand in hand they walked soberly home.

In the cottage sitting room Mr Bennett was looking through some papers. Mrs Bennett was looking out of the window.

"The weather really has changed at last," she said, as the children came in. "Hannah might go to the beach with them tomorrow, dear, don't you think?"

Mr Bennett nodded and turned over a page.

"I wonder what Hannah will think of our beach! She should enjoy that. Mike, you will explain to her about tides and things, won't you?"

Mr Bennett looked up. "What things?" he asked drily.

"Oh, you know, about not going over to the island when the tide's coming in, in case she can't get back. And not to bathe at the point when the tide's going out, and to watch out for deep holes—"

"Well, the children know all that," said Mr Bennett. "She'll be with them, won't she? I hadn't imagined her going off for a picnic on her own."

"No, of course not, but—"

"Then stop fussing, old dear. The world won't come to an end just because you're away for a day."

"A day and a half," Meg corrected.

"A day and a half then." Mr Bennett turned back to his papers.

"Oh, and we must remember to tell Hannah to take a jersey if she's going to the beach," said Mrs Bennett, "but not to wear slacks, or shoes and socks."

Mr Bennett nodded without looking up. "I'll remember. Nothing but a jersey."

"No, *not* nothing but a jersey." Mrs Bennett raised her eyes in mild despair. "Just to explain that she'll have to paddle across the creek so it's no use wearing anything that'll get wet. Shorts, if she has them, or a short skirt."

Mr Bennett looked up with a tired smile. "Do you want *me* to go through her wardrobe? Really, Judy, you're fussing too much. You can tell her all these things yourself before tomorrow. There's plenty of time."

"There isn't!" cried Mrs Bennett, her voice rising. "You keep saying that about everything, there's plenty of time! But there isn't, that's the point. There's no time. Goodness knows what'll happen when it comes to moving—" She stopped in mid-sentence and turned back to the window. Meg looked up sharply. There was a sudden silence in the room.

"Moving what?" asked Meg.

Mr Bennett thrust his papers aside with an impatient movement.

"Moving nothing. Nobody's moving anything. Mummy's in a state because she thinks no one can manage here for a day and a half without her, that's all."

"She didn't mean us moving, did she?"

"Moving house, you mean?" He brushed the question aside. "I don't know what she meant. But if we do move I'll let you know well beforehand. That's a promise. At the moment we're supposed to be on holiday here. I'm supposed to be looking through these papers. And Mummy's trying to sort things out for tomorrow. Is that quite clear? So run away, there's a good girl. And don't go getting funny ideas."

Mrs Bennett turned back from the window with her usual smile.

"Yes, that's right. You had a nice time out, did you, darlings? Did you meet anyone we know?"

"No." Meg hesitated. "But we saw Mrs Jarvis."

"Oh?" A shadow crossed her mother's face. "You didn't go down the little lane, I hope?"

"No. She was in the road, quite a long way down."

"Really? I didn't think she ever went so far." Mrs Bennett frowned slightly. "You do know not to go down the little lane, don't you, darling? It does say it's a private road."

"Yes, I know. We don't."

"Good. Well, run along now. We must let Daddy get on. And I must start getting my things ready for tomorrow."

3

Hannah's Trouble

Meg awoke early next day and heard her parents already moving about. They would be leaving as soon as breakfast was over. Feeling there must be things she wanted to say to them before they went—though she could not think what—she got up and went into their room.

Maxie was already there, staring moodily out of the window. Her mother was at the dressing table, brushing her hair.

"What is it, darling?" said Mrs Bennett. "Maxie, do go and get dressed now, or else go back to bed."

"Nothing special," said Meg, racking her brains for some intelligent question she could ask. "You did say four from the milkman, didn't you? But what if we don't use them all?"

"Not to worry," said Mrs Bennett. "I can make a milk pudding tomorrow evening. There won't be time for it to go sour."

"Yes, we'll be back before you know we've gone," said Mr Bennett with a forced little laugh. "You will be a good girl and look after things here, won't you?"

Meg saw suddenly that he was worried, trying not to

show it. (About Granny Bennett perhaps—not just his interview?)

"Yes, we'll be all right," she said quickly. "I hope Granny Bennett won't—" she was going to say 'die' but stopped herself in the nick of time—"won't be wearing that awful old brown cardigan," she said.

"What on earth are you talking about?" said her mother sharply. "Now do run away and get dressed. At once."

Maxie was silent at breakfast and would not eat.

"Sweetheart, what *is* it?" said Mrs Bennett, holding a loaded spoon against his closed mouth. "What's the matter?"

Maxie ducked sideways. "I *told* you," he mumbled, kicking the table leg. "I want to go to Nanny T's."

"But sweetheart, we can't go *today*, I told you. We're going to London. When we come back, I promise."

Nanny T was the first person the children always went to see when they came on holiday. Her real name was Mrs Thompson, and long ago when Mrs Bennett herself was a child and had come there for holidays, had sat in with her at nights when her parents were out. That was when she had first been called Nanny T, and Meg and Maxie had never thought of her by any other name.

"She'll be wanting to see me," Maxie insisted.

"Of course she will," said Mrs Bennett, "and so she shall. But it's been so wet, and there's been so much to do. There hasn't been time yet."

Meg frowned. Maxie going on and on about Nanny T always irritated her. She didn't belong to him. Nanny T liked seeing them both.

Mr Bennett was suggesting Hannah might go with

them. He could explain to her how to get there, and the children knew the way. Had she understood what they were saying? Would she like to go?

Hannah nodded, all smiles. She was a lot happier since Mrs Bennett had explained to her about the post, and she was confidently expecting her letter any day now. Yes, she would enjoy to go. The children should show her the way. She was happy to have understood everything. She would have a nice time. And she would see to everything.

"And just in *case* of an emergency, you know where to go," Mrs Bennett said. ('Emergency' was a new word which Hannah was pleased to have learnt.) Yes, that too, she understood.

"I am happy to exercise this word," she said, and pink with pleasure smiled on them all.

Mrs Bennett turned to Meg. "Let Maxie take his kite if you do go to Nanny T's. He wants to show it to her. You can help him carry it." She glanced at Maxie. "What is it, sweetheart? Why are you shaking your head?"

"I don't want to take it."

"But why not?"

"It might get broken," Maxie mumbled, his head bent.

"Broken? Why should it get broken? Meg will carry it for you, I told you."

Meg stared at Maxie, holding her breath. If he was going to tell . . . Anyway she hadn't meant it, he knew that. It was only that he'd been so irritating about it the other day, not letting her have a go, and dawdling, and carrying on as if it was so immensely important which way up she carried it. And of course she hadn't broken it. Why should she want to break a silly old kite? She wouldn't have wanted one herself even if they'd thought of buying her one. There hadn't been anything she wanted in the village shop anyway. They only sold things like little plastic prams for girls, and baby toys she was far too old for.

Mr Bennett looked at his watch. "Well, it's time we were off. Got everything?"

"Yes, I think so. Have a nice time anyway, darlings. And I'll be back tomorrow. After tea, I expect."

There was a quick rush round for coats, case, handbag, then goodbyes at the door, and they were off.

It was very quiet when they had driven away. Maxie had disappeared round the back of the cottage. Hannah was upstairs making the beds. Still standing on the doorstep, Meg waited for the empty feeling of saying goodbye to pass. Then she looked across towards the sea. There was a slight haze over the marsh. In the nearer field, cows were grazing in the early morning sunshine. Only one person was in sight, the postman pedalling along the distant track towards Rook Hall.

Her heart lifted suddenly. The postman might have Hannah's letter with him. That would make her happy again. And it was beach weather at last! They could go there on their way to Nanny T's, show Hannah their lovely, wonderful beach, with miles and miles of sand, and seagulls and oyster catchers, and millions of shells just waiting to be picked up. They would all have a lovely day.

And until they went to Nanny T's Maxie would be all hers—hers to look after, and make a fuss of if he needed it. Hannah didn't count, because Maxie mumbled sometimes and then she couldn't understand what he said. But Meg could. She understood him. He was her little brother after all. She warmed towards him, remembering how he hadn't told at breakfast about the kite. And yet he had seemed to take it seriously, silly boy. Where was he now?

As she turned to look for him, he came slowly round the side of the house, dragging his feet, looking utterly dejected. He came and stood beside her silently on the step.

"I won't break your silly old kite," she said gently.

He shook his head but still looked miserable.

"They'll be back tomorrow, you know."

"I know." He brushed the remark aside as if it was irrelevant.

"We'll go and buy mint lumps, shall we?" Again he shook his head. "Why not? You know you like them. I'll pay."

He did not answer.

It struck her now that he had been funny ever since last night, not talking, refusing his biscuits at bedtime, staring mournfully at nothing in the bath. And then suddenly wanting to see Nanny T like that. He would always tell her things he wouldn't tell anyone else.

"What's the matter?" she asked.

"Nothing."

She heard the ping of a bicycle bell and realized the postman was coming up the lane. He would be jolly with Maxie, perhaps offer him a ride on the saddle, make jokes with him. It was always like that. But if something was wrong with Maxie she was entitled to know what. It was not for the postman to make him happy if he had turned down her offer of mint lumps.

She pulled him round to the back of the cottage.

"Now tell me, what's the matter?" He was silent. "You'd better tell me."

He hesitated, then came closer and mumbled something so low she could scarcely hear the words. She bent down to him.

"You *what?*"

"I killed a frog."

"When?"

"Yesterday. After tea."

"Why?"

"I don't know."

"How?"

"I got a stick and hit it. It sort of squeaked, and then it sort of burst, and I went on hitting it." He stared at her wretchedly. "I don't know what to do."

She was silent, deeply shocked, thinking how awful; surely he ought to be punished for doing something so dreadful?

She said slowly, "You'll have to tell."

"Will I?"

"Yes, of course."

"But they aren't here."

She wondered if he should tell Hannah. But it was not the sort of thing Hannah could be told. This was something their parents ought to know about. They would know what sort of punishment he ought to have.

"We'll have to wait till they get back," she said. He began to cry, helplessly, wretchedly. She took his hand.

"Never mind. Poor little frog, but never mind." He clung to her and she felt warm and comforting. He was so different like this, needing her. And no one but she could protect and comfort him. "Don't cry. I'll look after you. We'll think of something nice to do today, shall we?"

"Go to Nanny T's?" He looked up, perhaps a little too eagerly.

She grew solemn. "I don't know. We'll have to see."

"She likes me coming," he said, his voice quivering.

"I know. But going to Nanny T's is more like a treat, isn't it?" He knew at once what she meant. He didn't deserve a treat today. "Perhaps we'll go to the beach, though. That'll be nearly as nice, won't it?"

He nodded.

"Then we'll go there. We'll forget all about the poor little frog and go to the beach and have a nice time there. But you must be a good boy."

He nodded gratefully, still holding her hand.

"And perhaps, if you're a *very* good boy we might go to Nanny T's on the way back. But I can't promise."

Of course she could not promise. Once they got to Nanny T's he would be hers no longer. Nanny T had always specially loved Maxie—it was no good her pretending not to know that—and he would be pampered and cosied and made a fuss of, the way he always was . . . But he needed cosying now, she thought, looking down at him, with his face all crumply and smudged like that. And he was so little. Little and thin, like a bird without feathers. She put an arm round his shoulders.

"I can't *promise*," she said again, "but we'll see." And she squeezed him close to her side, the way their mother did, and they went indoors.

But once there, they stopped in amazement. Hannah was sitting at the kitchen table with her letter in her hand, and she was crying, actually crying, the way Maxie cried, without even a handkerchief to mop up the tears.

"Whatever's the matter?" said Meg in a flat shocked voice.

"My brudder, my brudder," sobbed Hannah. "Oh Gott!"

"What's happened to him?"

"My brudder—tomorrow he get married! *Tomorrow*—and here I am!" She stared at them with streaming eyes.

Embarrassed, Meg stared at the floor while she took in the full awfulness of the news. Hannah would miss the wedding! Her eye fell on something under the table, a paper that must have fallen from the envelope. She bent and picked it up. Hannah seized it and stared at it through her tears.

"Mein Gott! It is my air ticket—my air ticket!" and she burst into fresh sobs. "My mudder she send me ticket to go home—" she looked again at the envelope—"but she send it to London and it come too late. My brudder, he get married quick. Heidi's mudder, she say he must. Oh, my Gott!"

Meg was still shocked. Hannah crying was an alarming sight. She choked and sobbed until it almost seemed as if she might drown in her own tears. And yet she was grown up. "I'll get you a handkerchief," she said, and went across to the paper towel roll hanging on the door. Thinking hard, she tore off four sheets and handed them to Hannah, one at a time.

"When would you have to go?" she asked slowly, "to get there in time?"

"Today. *Today!* And it is not possible."

"Are you sure?" said Meg, still thinking.

"I cannot leave you!"

"We *could* manage," said Meg uncertainly.

No, it was quite impossible, Hannah said. Meg must not try to persuade her; she would never leave the children. They were not babies, of course—but then she had promised Mrs Bennett. There was no question of it; she would never let her down.

Hannah stared out of the window.

If she could find a lady to look after them perhaps . . . But no. She had said she would. She was quite firm about it. She was determined.

It was only when she thought of the pink rose on the hat that was to match her dress that she gave in altogether. She would go. She *must* go.

"The lady with the telephone," she said, "this truly an emergency is—she will look after you, yes?"

"No," said Meg firmly. "Not her." That at least she was sure about. "I tell you what though, we *could* go to Nanny T's. We were going there anyway. She'd look after us."

"Oh yes!" said Maxie.

"And she has beds? That is good."

"Not—" Maxie began, but Meg pinched him gently while Hannah blew her nose. He looked up, puzzled. "But there's only . . ."

"Plenty," said Meg firmly. Anything, she thought, rather than have Mrs Jarvis come here. Or worse, if she and Maxie should have to spend the night at Rook Hall!

"And you see we can easily go on our own. She only

lives the other side of the village," Meg assured her, not mentioning how far the other side. "It's near Nettleton marsh. We've been there hundreds of times on our way back from the beach. But you'll have to hurry, Hannah, if you're going to catch the London train."

Hannah needed no more persuading.

"Then I will pack you little case, yes?"

No, there was really no need, Meg told her, but Hannah insisted, even carrying it downstairs and putting it by the front door.

"So! For you all is now ready," she said, and dashed upstairs to pack her own.

But how was she to get to the station? They had not thought of that. It was more than ten miles away, much too far to walk. They were racking their brains over the problem—a bicycle they might borrow? A possible lift? Even walking along the main road and holding up a passing car––only that would take too long, Hannah moaned, relapsing into tears again—when they heard the clink of milk bottles below.

"It's Mr Duffy, the milkman!" cried Meg. "Go and ask him."

Hannah stumbled down the stairs, the others followed, and in a bunch they ran to the door. He was already there.

"You say," said Hannah.

"No, you," said Meg.

"*Please!*" they gasped together.

The milkman looked from one to the other with a smile.

"Another pint? I've left you the usual four." They havered, each waiting for the other to speak.

Maxie wormed his way out. "I'll say." He cleared

his throat, looked earnestly at the milkman, and said all in one breath: "Please Mr Duffy will you take this lady to the station she won't a bit mind riding with the milk bottles but she's got to catch a train." He glanced at Meg for approval and stepped back.

"Well I never!" said Mr Duffy. He put down his crate and pushed his cap to the back of his head. "The station? But that's right out of my way, laddie." He looked at Meg, then at Hannah, her face red with anxiety, swollen with tears. "Is something wrong, m'dear?"

"Such trouble am I in!" Hannah blurted out.

"I am sorry to hear that," he said seriously, and really looked it.

"Yes," said Meg, "she's got to go to a wedding in Germany today. It's terribly important for her."

"A wedding, eh? Well, it wouldn't do to miss a wedding, I do understand that. But today!"

"Well, actually the wedding's tomorrow, but she's got to go today. And we don't know how to get her to the station."

"My ticket I have! Tonight will I fly!" Hannah spread her arms wide in a gesture of despair—and even in the middle of all her confusion and concern a picture flashed across Meg's mind of Hannah flapping her way across the Channel on wings. She turned to the milkman.

"You see, my parents are out, and she's only just heard it's to be tomorrow."

He looked surprised, then serious. "I tell you what," he said. "Why not phone Mr Sutton over in Barnham? He runs a taxi."

Meg explained that they were not on the phone.

Then an idea struck her. "But Mrs Jarvis is. At Rook Hall. Are you going there?"

"No." He shook his head and his face seemed to close up. "No. I don't go there no more." There was a moment's silence. "Nor you neither, I shouldn't think," he muttered under his breath.

Then his face cleared. He had thought of the answer. It was quite simple. In ten minutes or so he would be passing the taximan's house, and he would ask him to come straight away. How would that do?

"Oh yes! Thank you very much," said Meg.

"You are so good!" said Hannah, now almost sobbing with relief.

"Well, m'dear, it seems you've left it a bit late, but that's nowt to do with me. Happy landings, as they say, and—" he smiled and made her a little bow—"I'll take this opportunity to wish you every happiness in your future life."

It was only when he had gone, after shaking hands warmly with Hannah and waving them all goodbye, that Meg wondered whether he had thought it was Hannah's own wedding she was in such a hurry to get to. If so, she hoped it wouldn't have made any difference. But she could explain to him tomorrow about the pink dress and Hannah being bridesmaid and everything. He seemed an understanding sort of man.

She ran upstairs to help Hannah, who was now emptying the drawers in her room, throwing all her possessions into two suitcases with trembling hands.

"I must make hurry!" Hannah gasped, "but I cannot think. I am all washed up."

Meg urged her on. It seemed now as important to her as to Hannah that she should not miss the wedding.

"My dress is there ready, like I told you," said Hannah. "The wedding was for October fixed. Why they make it now I do not know." She wept again, suddenly remembering she was leaving the children, then hurried on with her packing, and twenty minutes later the taximan was knocking at the door.

Hannah left in a muddle of tears and excitement. "You are so good children, you will be good, yes? Your poor mudder! I beg her pardon for this adventure. I hope she will forgive. But ah, the wedding! Heidi, she is so pewtiful, and I am to be bridesmaid! I am sad to go, but oh so happy!"

She almost fell into the taxi and was driven away waving, smiling, sobbing, all at the same time.

Meg and Maxie looked at each other. "Well, she's gone," said Meg, and took their little case upstairs again. Maxie followed. In the bedroom she began unpacking their night things. Maxie stared.

"But aren't we going to Nanny T's?"

"Don't be silly, we can't go and *stay* there. Where would we sleep? Anyway, she's too old. I'm sure they wouldn't want us to go there and *ask* to stay. They'd expect us to stay here and—and be sensible, and good." She was slightly worried but trying not to show it.

"Then why did you say we'd go?"

She rounded on him sharply. "Didn't you *hear*? She was going to ask Mrs Jarvis. How would you like that, stay a night with a witch? Or have to go and stay at her house?"

That silenced him. Meg put their pyjamas back on the beds and went downstairs to see what there was to eat. There was sliced ham in the fridge, and eggs and tomatoes, and a veal and ham pie still in its paper wrapping. With bread and jam and Marmite that should be plenty. And the milkman had left four pints. She brought them in and put them in the fridge. She was beginning to feel efficient and competent. It was only for one night. They would manage very well.

4

In Memory of a Frog

"When are we going to the beach?" said Maxie.

"In a minute. I'm just thinking," said Meg.

They were sitting at the kitchen table, having had a mug of milk, the sliced ham, and two biscuits each. "Then we shan't be hungry on the beach," Meg had said, proud of her motherly forethought. But now she had been sitting silent, frowning at the table top for nearly five minutes, and Maxie was growing impatient.

"Why can't we go now?"

"Because I'm thinking. I told you."

"What about?"

She turned on him impatiently. "About Mrs Jarvis, if you want to know."

He looked apprehensive. "What about her? She won't come here, will she?"

No, Meg was sure she wouldn't. What was on her mind was whether it was now safe to go past the little lane on their way to the creek. In the past, wondering whether Mrs Jarvis would be there had always made a small excitement in their walks along the coast road. But now it was different.

"You see," she said, "she never used to go so far down the road before—she's supposed to be isolated—and she never *said* anything before, did she? I think we ought to be specially careful now we're all by ourselves."

He nodded in solemn agreement, but could not resist asking: "What might she do?"

Meg thought. Should she say she might have some power to draw us into her house, and then put a spell on us or something—which was what she had been thinking? No, she only said things like that when she was annoyed with him. Today she was looking after him.

"Oh, I don't know," she said. "Don't let's bother. We'll go through the village instead, and down past the farm."

"Oh goody! Past the stream."

It was a much longer way to go. She had been wondering whether it was too far, and was relieved when he accepted the idea without question. "Get your jersey then."

"Must I? I don't want to wear it."

"Tie it round you, then. You'll need it later. The wind's fresher on the beach, as you well know. We don't want you catching cold."

He looked up at her, awe and admiration in his eyes. "You sound just like Mummy."

Flattered, but ignoring the remark, she bustled around, swilling the mugs under the tap, putting the biscuit tin away, and collecting their jerseys and sand-shoes. "Do you want your spade?"

"Do I have to carry it?"

She slipped it under her own arm with an air of good

humoured resignation. Again just like Mummy. How easy it seemed.

"And Pokey!" said Maxie.

Pokey was a small white cloth rabbit which Maxie adored but Meg found unsympathetic. His black button eyes gave him a silly surprised look, she thought. In fact she really rather hated Pokey; he was so exclusively Maxie's, and everyone else took him so seriously. But her mother always carried him in her bag when asked. She would not be outdone. With a smile she rolled him up in her jersey in a tight bundle and put that, too, under her arm.

She began to feel happy. Mrs Jarvis was disposed of. Hannah would have caught her train. And she and Maxie were going to have a lovely time at the beach all on their own. At the door she paused, considered, then locked it and pocketed the key.

Maxie ran ahead along the track to the village, his jersey, tied round his waist by the sleeves, flapping behind him like a little apron. She walked behind, thinking how small and sweet he looked, and promised herself she would be kind to him all day. Now Hannah had gone he was all hers. She would look after him properly. And he would be grateful and loving and sweet, the way he was with Nanny T and all the other grown ups.

It was really rather jolly without Hannah. Nice as she was, it had been a bit of a drag having to go everywhere with her, and explain about things, and wonder if she was happy. Now she was free—to pick a few poppies, to stand watching a lapwing as it strutted along the edge of a cornfield, even—when a seagull, brilliantly white against the blue sky, swerved past her head—to say suddenly, out loud, "Oh lovely, lovely!" without having to explain why. She ran to catch Maxie up.

Appealingly he put his hand in hers. "Tell me a story."

She told him the story of Hansel and Gretel, thinking to point the contrast in their situations and make him feel safe and looked after. Hansel and Gretel had been sent away, but they had not. Hansel and Gretel had come to the witch's house, but they had come the opposite way. Hansel and Gretel were in danger, but Maxie was not because Meg was looking after him. Maxie smiled to himself and looked quite smug.

She made the story get frightening (after all it was meant to be, wasn't it?) and he shuddered happily and said, "Go on." But when she came to the witch part and he asked, a little nervously: "What was she like?" she couldn't resist saying, "Like Mrs Jarvis."

She saw the fear leap into his eyes but went on relentlessly (well, you couldn't stop a story in the middle), "And then the witch said to Gretel in a deep growly voice *why didn't you let him choose the way?* And Gretel said I did. This was the way he chose. Then the witch said oh goody, and with a terrible gr-r-rowl she dragged him into the house. You've been a naughty boy, she said, I know what you've done and I'm going to punish you. I shall put you in a cage and fatten you up to eat—"

Maxie put his hands over his ears. "No, stop. I don't want to hear any more."

"It's got a happy end." Meg saw his face quivering, near to tears. She pressed on quickly. "So the witch gave him lots and lots to eat so he should get fatter and fatter, and every day she came and said—"

"No. Safe me, Meg!" Maxie cried.

She relented. "All right, I'll 'safe' you." She stopped and put her arms round him. "There's nothing to be frightened of. You're quite safe with me. I'll look after you."

"Promise?"

"Yes, of course."

How sweet he was! And how much he needed her! She hugged him tightly, glowing with warmth and loving kindness, and in a while he recovered. But it was right he should be frightened of Mrs Jarvis, she told herself as they set off again. It wouldn't be safe not to be.

Maxie walked close beside her, happy again but subdued.

"Are you tired yet?" Meg asked.

"Not much."

"We'll play I-spy, shall we? We'll get there quicker then."

They played I-spy all the way to the village. Mrs Wegg at the door of the bakery smiled as they passed. "Off to the beach, are you?" Maxie waved and said they were. He loved being recognized. "That's right. Be a good little old boy and do what big sister tells you." She turned to an older woman coming out of the shop. "Lucky kids, eh? Not a care in the world!"

"Well, I should hope not, yet," said the woman sourly, glancing after them.

Maxie looked up at Meg with a pleased smile. "She called you big sister."

"Well, I am, aren't I?"

"Yes. Who was the grumpy lady?"

"Mrs Pacey."

"Oh. I don't think she likes people."

They passed the mill and came to the little stream that ran along the side of the road. Here Maxie broke away from her and ran joyfully ahead. He ducked under the low railing, calling her to come and see. The water was quite shallow and very clear. Clumps of forget-me-nots grew along the bank, and brightly coloured stones and weeds shimmered in the sunlight below the rippling running water.

Usually Meg turned a few somersaults over the railing, but today she stood watching Maxie. He edged along the bank towards a dark green clump of weed. "Look, Meg, watercress!" and reached out to pick a handful.

"Careful now. You don't want to fall in."

"It isn't deep."

"I know, but we don't want any *more* washing," she said primly.

He looked over his shoulder and laughed delightedly. "*You* don't do the washing!" But she had not meant it to be funny. He waved the sprigs of watercress at her. "Hooray, watercress for tea! Clever me!"

"It's probably poisonous," she said coldly. "You've got to buy watercress in shops. Everybody knows that."

He came back to the road and, to tease her, held the bunch in front of his mouth. His eyes laughed at her over the top.

"What if I did eat it?"

She lunged forward, grabbed it from him, and flung it back into the stream. Then she turned her back on him and walked on.

Knowing he would be following, she made herself

tall, walking with her head well up, turning from side
to side to admire the view. Every now and then she
raised a hand to shield her eyes from the sun and gazed
into the distance. Occasionally she stopped, one hand
on her hip, head thrown back, to inspect the leaf of
some particular tree (actually to make sure out of the
corner of her eye that he was not far behind). She heard
him chuckle, and turned sharply.

"What's so funny?"

"You. Trying to look like Mummy." He laughed
out loud, crowing, and imitated her, his spiky little legs
mincing along the road, his mouth pursed up, one hand
over his eyes. Then she saw that he was still holding a
sprig of the watercress.

"Give that to me!"

"No!"

He held it behind his back, then waved it with a
flourish and deliberately put it to his mouth.

"All right, *get* poisoned!" Meg shouted. "I expect
you will, and I'll be glad."

Meg walked on, no longer looking at the view.
Absurdly, there were tears in her eyes. Why was it so
difficult to be kind to him all the time?

This morning, when he had been telling her about
the frog, it had been so easy to be kind. And yet it was a
dreadful thing he had done. She couldn't imagine
doing such a thing herself. And how could he be so
happy now? Could he have forgotten already? Had she
let him think it didn't matter?

He had caught her up and was skipping along beside

her, smiling up at her every time he caught her eye. Surely he shouldn't look quite so happy yet?

"I did eat a bit of that watercress," he said, and she saw there was a gleam of triumph in his eye. She ignored the remark. "Will I die?"

"Probably."

She sensed his sudden doubt and saw him drop back. So he really had! She turned round.

"How much?"

"Only a leaf. It was in my mouth and now it isn't, so I must have swallowed it."

Relieved, she said, "That'll be all right," and his face cleared.

"Shall we play I-spy again?" he asked. That was to placate her, she knew.

"Not just yet," she said sadly.

"Why not?"

"I'm thinking."

"About the watercress?"

"No."

"Mrs Jarvis?"

"No."

"What about?"

"The little frog." She saw his smile fade. "I hope it didn't hurt him too much." He was silent. "Don't you?"

He gave a little gasp, then said quickly: "I think he had tears in his eyes—just for a minute—that's why I hit him again—quickly."

"Oh, Maxie!"

He made to run from her, but she grabbed his arm. "You are sorry now, aren't you?" He wriggled silently with his head down. "Say you are," she insisted.

He looked up, speechless, and she saw with relief that he was about to cry again. So he had not forgotten. He did mind. He wrenched his arm away suddenly and stood a few feet away from her, rubbing it.

"That hurt," he said. "You pinched me."

She let that pass. He was probably only pretending. They walked on in silence for a while, and turned down the little road to the creek. It was the lunch hour and hardly anyone was about. Seagulls cried over the marsh, and in the distance they could hear the sighing sound of the sea.

"We could have given him a funeral," Meg said in a sad voice. "We should have. Then he'd have known you were sorry. Without a funeral it seems as if you aren't, doesn't it?"

"Does it?"

"It does to me."

He looked mournful. "We can't. I threw him over the hedge." A tear rolled down his cheek. He licked it up sideways and sniffed.

"Never mind, we'll have a pretend funeral, shall we?"

He thought about this, then nodded. "How?"

"We'll make a little grave and pick flowers to put on it."

He looked interested. "Go on."

"And we could make a standy-up stone to stick in the top."

"Oh yes! What of?"

She thought. Cardboard wouldn't do. It would get wet in the rain. "I know! We could look for a flat stone on the beach. A big white one."

"Oh yes! Good you got my spade." He rubbed his

hands with satisfaction. "Sometimes the best ones are just under the sand."

He had cheered up completely, and ran down to the creek as excited as if they were going to search for treasure instead of a tombstone.

Here they would have to paddle across to the marsh to get to the island. They sat on the side of a dinghy to take off their sandshoes.

"And when we've found the stone," said Meg, "we could write something on it like they do in the churchyard."

Maxie looked up brightly, wagging his head. "What sort of thing?"

"Well, Rest in Peace, or Gone to Heaven—"

He chuckled suddenly. "Gone to Heaven. Back in a minute. That's what Mrs Wegg puts on the shop door when she's gone to see her dinner isn't burning." He laughed, hugging himself, and nearly fell over backwards into the boat.

Meg hauled him up furiously. "It isn't. It *isn't*! Her house isn't called Heaven. It's called *Haven*, you silly boy."

But it was no use. The more she scolded him, the more Maxie laughed until he was in a really silly mood.

"Gone to Heaven. Back in a minute. Would he come flying, do you think?" He laughed uproariously. "What does a frog look like with wings? And with a white dress like a angel?" She slapped him suddenly on the leg. It was more than she could bear. The laughter left his face as suddenly as it had come. He rubbed his leg and said sullenly, "That's two things now."

"What d'you mean, two things?"

"You hurt my arm and now you've hurt my leg."

He slipped off the boat and stood on one leg, holding the other. "Now I can't walk."

"Yes, you can. Don't be silly."

He hopped a step or two, lost his balance and fell over sideways. "Serves you right," said Meg, and left him to pick himself up. But this time he had hurt himself. He had cut his leg on a stone and blood was running freely down to his ankle.

Alarmed, she dabbed at it with her handkerchief. Happily, it was not too bad after all, but the shock had made her angry. She no longer felt like comforting him.

She tied the handkerchief round his leg and carried him across the creek. His feet trailed in the water because she was not tall enough to hold him clear. He whined, "It's cold!"

"I can't help that," she gasped. She was breathless. He was heavier than he looked. On the far side she put him down. "You can walk now."

He stood whimpering on the shore. "I want to go to Nanny T's."

"Well, you can't."

"Yes, I can."

"No, you can't. Not till they come back."

The corners of his mouth turned down. "I want to go to Nanny T's."

"Not till they come back, I tell you. And then only if you're good. I'll tell them if you aren't. Now why don't you shut up?"

They trailed across the marsh through patches of mud and samphire, Maxie's wails mingling with the cries of seagulls. "I'm tired, I'm tire-ed."

"Too bad."

He lagged behind. "I want a wee."

"Have a wee then."

"Will you wait?"

"I might."

She walked slowly on, looking ahead to where the island lay bathed in sunshine. It was often like that. On the marsh there would be ever changing light and shade as clouds chased each other across the enormous sky. But the island would remain sunlit—like an enchanted place.

Maxie caught her up, panting. "You didn't wait."

"I only said I might. What was there to wait for?"

"I told you. I'm tired. I can't walk."

"Yes, you can. If you don't stop winnicking I'll go on and leave you." 'Winnicking' was Nanny T's word for whimpering. It reminded him.

"I want to go to Nanny T's," he wailed again. Then, as she carried out her threat and began running, "No-o! No-o-o! No-o-o!"

His plaintive wail grew fainter as she ran from him, away over the marsh, jumping the tiny streams, skirting the muddy patches, until she came to the stretch of sea lavender. Looking back she saw him, a small dark blob in the distance. She stooped to pick some of the dry prickly flowers, and was surrounded by silence; only the sound of water running in the narrow streams, and one skylark trilling higher and higher away up overhead. For the moment it almost seemed as if time had stopped.

5

Alone in the Sandhills

By the time Maxie had caught her up, and they had paddled across the far end of the creek to the island, Meg breathed a sigh of relief. At least they had got here. At last. Now they must enjoy themselves. Surely nobody could be on the island and not enjoy themselves.

They found a hollow in the sand dunes, on the side that looked out to sea. Meg unrolled her jersey, handed Pokey to Maxie—who greeted him with an exaggerated pleasure that irritated her—and produced the two cream biscuits she had brought as a treat. (Why hadn't she brought four?) Maxie looked at them, unimpressed, as if they were ordinary ginger biscuits.

"Is that all?"

"Those are extra." She frowned. He must enjoy himself now at all costs. "You can have mine if you like." He still looked unsatisfied.

"If we went to Nanny T's she'd give us bread and sugar," he remarked. "And a drink of tea."

"I know, but we can't. Not today, it's too far. What about looking for that stone now? You can have first look if you like." She held out his spade. "Only don't paddle. The waves are too big." But he had lost interest. "Why not?" He wouldn't say. "You thought it was a good idea before."

"Well, I don't now. I want to go to Nanny T's."

He looked up at her under his eyelashes with such a baleful glare that she lost all patience.

"Well, you can't, so there. And I shouldn't think they'll let you tomorrow either, because you haven't been good."

"I *have!*" He kicked the sand up with his foot and it splayed over her.

"You haven't." She brushed the sand from her face. "Anyway you don't deserve to go," she said, with meaning. "You know why."

His eyes grew suddenly wary. He scrambled to his feet.

"I *don't* know!" he shouted, and darted away from her, over the bank and down the other side.

She was furious, with herself and him. She had reminded him once too often. Now he was getting used to it. The day she had planned—the day that was to have been so happy, when she was to have been so kind and patient, so much more kind and patient, she felt, than anyone had ever been with her—the day was spoilt. It had gone all wrong. She could not set it right now even if she wanted to.

Angrily she stood up and shouted over the sandhill: "You probably will die if you've eaten that leaf! I hope you do!"

There was no sign of him. Hiding probably. He would have heard. She sat down again, scowling, and sat hugging her knees, staring out to sea, still hearing her words hanging in the air—*you probably will die . . . I hope you do . . .*

The seagulls mewed and screamed along the beach, the wind sighed in the marram grass, and now Meg was walking slowly in a white dress, carrying a simple sheaf of poppies and corn, picked by herself, to lay on Maxie's grave in the village churchyard . . . A tear stole down her cheek.

No, that was silly thinking. Maxie wasn't dead, he was only a stupid little boy.

What about Granny Bennett then—Granny Bennett who 'wasn't very well?' It had flashed into her mind earlier on that she might be really ill and they were not saying so. She had forgotten about it later, with the excitement about Hannah and everything. But now, with the day gone all wrong, it had become another thing to worry about.

Granny Bennett had never been their favourite granny. With her ready frown and her quick, abrupt way of talking (and the awful brown cardigan) she wasn't an easy person to love. But it would be terrible if anything happened to her. It would feel like her fault for not having liked her much. *Might* she die?

If she did, she supposed she would gradually become one of those olden days people, all dead-and-gone, that Nanny T had talked about when they had once walked through the churchyard. 'Now don't you go jumping on them graves, Maxie.' 'Why not, Nanny T? Are there people there?' 'Yes, my beauty, olden days people, all dead-and-gone, but you mustn't jump on them.'

Or might Granny Bennett become a ghost? Oh, she hoped not! Not a spurious ghost . . . She didn't want to think of that . . .

There was still that other worry, vague and un-
formed, that she could only think of as 'it', because
she did not really know what it was. Something to do
with moving, she was pretty sure now—but also
something that concerned her personally. It was one of
those grown up things you could only guess at; something they would stop talking about when you came
into the room—and you only knew that because they
looked at you with more interest than usual, seeming
to concentrate on you for no particular reason; but
smiling, perhaps for fear you might ask what was up. It
was something to do with her personally, she knew.
Her mother had been making her a new dress. Instead
of putting the zip down the back, she had made it in the
front, saying it might be handy to have dresses you
could do up yourself if you were away from home. It
had struck Meg then that perhaps she was going to be
sent away somewhere—surely not to boarding
school?—But when she had asked outright her mother
had laughed and said no, of course not. "Then why
might I be away from home?" Meg had asked, and her
mother had said, "Well, you always might go and stay
with someone, mightn't you?" And she had laughed
again, calling her a little worrier and suspicious, so
Meg had said no more. But she had grown watchful,
listening . . .

Yes, perhaps she *had* grown suspicious. She had been
worried about that appointment with Dr. Miller.
Awful possibilities had leapt into her mind—her
mother was going to be ill, go into hospital, perhaps
die—but she knew now that was nonsense. Her
mother had said so, and her mother never told lies.
Anyway, it was something different, to do with home,

but what? The thought nagged at her. Why wouldn't they *say*?

She remembered a few nights ago, when she was supposed to be asleep, her mother coming up to bed. She was saying something about Maxie. "Maxie could always go to Nanny T's," she had said. "It's Meg I'm worried about." Meg had woken up properly then, and heard her father's patient voice replying, "Don't worry, old girl, it'll all probably work out all right." Then they had shut the bedroom door.

So 'it,' whatever it was, would be all right for Maxie. Of course it would, she thought bitterly. But what about her?

Maxie—he still hadn't come back! Alarmed, she stood up and looked around. Not a sign of him. She climbed up the bank to get a better view and saw nothing but more sandhills, and marram grass blowing in the wind. In a hollow she came on one of his sand-shoes. She climbed a higher hill and saw, away to her left, a group of people walking with a dog. None of them was as small as Maxie. To her right, in the far distance, someone was dabbing for flatfish in the shallows. That was all. What could have happened to him?

The answer flashed into her mind almost before she had time to think it. He could be drowned. He could have gone down to paddle because she'd specially told him not to, and been swept away by the current; or more likely, knocked over by one of those big sluggish waves that rolled in looking so much smaller than they really were; and then, before he had time to struggle to his feet, been knocked over by another, and another . . .

No, of course he hadn't been drowned. She knew what had happened. He had set off by himself in the direction of Nanny T's cottage, paddling over the creek, crossing the sands towards Nettleton marsh; making out he was going there, though he knew it was much too far. He was doing it to frighten her. Well, she had better go after him.

She plunged down from the sandhills, splashed through the creek and away over the sands towards the marsh. He was nowhere in sight. He must have reached the dyke already and gone down the other side into the field. She ran faster, jumping over the narrow streams and muddy ditches, slithering through the samphire. When she reached the dyke she would be able to see him.

But there was no question of seeing Maxie from the dyke after all. A mist had fallen over the fields. She could barely see a yard ahead. She plunged down the bank through the long grass, running blind into the mist. Grazing cows loomed up like grey ghosts around her. Her hair grew damp and limp. Her jeans seemed to cling around her knees, making it difficult to run. The mist grew thicker and she stopped to get her bearings. Then a cow loomed up close beside her and startled her into a run again. Where was the stile? Which way?

She called: "Maxie! Maxie!"

Cold fear gripped her. Maxie was not here, nowhere in these fields. And he could never have got as far as this so quickly. Something awful had happened to him because she had wished him dead. She had said it out loud, *you probably will die . . . I hope you do*, and the words had gone on and on into space, and would be going on, further and further, for ever and ever. Panic seized her suddenly and she shouted again: "Maxie! Where are you? I didn't mean it!" But there was no answer, only a cow lowed and another answered from a further field. Then suddenly she was at the stile.

It appeared quite unexpectedly at her left hand, and she grasped the rough wood, slimy with damp and lichen, as if it were an old friend. Now at least she knew where she was. What a difference it made!

The panic left her as suddenly as it had come, and she sank down in the grass beside the stile. She felt hot and heavy with relief. How silly she had been! Of course Maxie was not anywhere here. He was still on the island; probably down at the sea side, searching for treasures on the tide line.

In a minute, when she'd had a rest, she would run back and find him—but just for the moment it was good to sit here, so limp and relaxed . . . She let her eyes close . . .

6

To the Dark House

Meg sat up with a start. She must have dozed off. For a moment she was not sure where she was, then she remembered. She was in the fields beyond Nettleton marsh, on the mainland, nearly halfway to Nanny T's cottage.

And Maxie was on the island! She must get back to him quickly. He would be wondering where she was. He had probably been hiding, just to tease her, and by now would be getting worried. She reached the shore and looked across to the island, hoping she might see him there, waving from a sandhill. But there was no sign. He would be back in their hollow.

Surely the creek was wider than it had been? It was. She could see it now. The tide must be coming in. She had thought it was running out, but she had only to wade into the water to feel it on her legs, pulling the other way, towards the marsh. It was coming in, and coming in fast the way it always did. She might be cut off!

The water was soon up to her knees. But it was only a little further now. How dreadful, though, if she had not got across in time! Maxie would have been left

alone on the island until the tide went down again,
three or four hours perhaps, all by himself. As it was,
there was barely time for the two of them to get back.
She must hurry, hurry!

The water grew shallower and she splashed ashore.

She ploughed up the steep slope to the sandhills, her
feet sinking into the soft dry sand which pulled her
back at every step. She reached the top and ran at once
to the hollow where they had been sitting. No Maxie.
No sign of him. She looked this way and that. Then
she went over the bank, and down to the beach. Again
no Maxie. Indeed, no one at all. As far as the eye could
see, on either side, the beach was empty.

Back she went to the sandhills again, running,
calling, trying all the while not to panic. But how could
she help it when she knew the tide was rising every
minute!

"Maxie, where *are* you? *Maxie!*"

Would she hear if he answered? She stood still and
listened. Only the soughing of the wind in the marram
grass, and the distant cry of a curlew away along the
beach.

She must be sensible. She would try the other side of
the island, the landward side. From there she would be
able to see across to the marsh. One glance was enough
to tell her that already it was too late. A wide sheet of
water separated the island from the mainland. Now
they would have to stay here, whether they liked it or
not, for several hours.

There was nothing to do but go back to the hollow.
If only she could find him sitting there! It wouldn't
matter then that they had to stay there for hours; they
would be together. But Maxie was not there, and she

began all over again, calling, listening, and calling again.

The wind was rising. The sea getting louder. Facing the sea, with the wind roaring in her ears, she thought she could hear him shouting for help. But when she turned her head sideways and there was sudden quiet, there were no shouts, no cries, only the wind whistling through the reeds, and the screaming of gulls on the beach.

She shivered. There would be more shelter down by the creek. She would go back to the place where later they would cross over to the mainland. That would be where he would expect to find her, once the tide had gone down. How many hours now? Two or three at least, she thought. It was not yet high water.

On the shore she came on footprints, barefooted, the toe marks showing sharply in the sand. They were smaller than hers. They could be his. They were heading towards the creek, becoming more and more distinct as they came to firmer sand.

She followed them down to the water's edge. Then her hand flew up to her mouth, and she stood there, trembling.

A sandshoe lay at the very edge, the flooding tide already lapping into it. And in it, sitting upright, with black, staring, button eyes, was Pokey.

For a moment Meg went blank. Then her mind raced. Footprints running down—Maxie's footprints—but *none coming back*. And Pokey still there. He would never have left him behind! She seized Pokey and held him close, searching his face for some clue. Never had his blank button eyes looked blanker. But she needed no clue. She knew what had happened.

Maxie had done what they always did—put his things down on the sand, then paddled a little way out to see if the water was shallow enough to cross. But the current had been too strong for him. It had swept him off his feet. And he had been drowned.

I wished him dead, she thought, despairing, and stumbled blindly up into the sandhills.

The wind came rushing in from the sea, flattening the marram grass, nearly blowing her off her feet. She shouted aloud: "Maxie! Come back! I didn't mean it!" but the words were torn from her mouth even before she could hear them. She tried again, screaming to hear her own voice: "Maxie, I didn't mean it! I didn't mean it!" But again the words were carried away. Where would they go? Would they, too, be going on and on into space, further and further, for ever and ever? If so, might he know? Oh, let him know! Please let him know! I didn't mean it! Again she shouted to the empty sky, and the wind seized her words and rushed away with them.

In a lull, she found a small hollow in a circle of reeds and crept inside. Out of the roar of the wind she grew calmer. Crouching in the sand she wept again at the thought of his little grave in the village churchyard— Maxie amongst all the olden days people up on the hillside, with the wind blowing the long grass, and her poppies on his grave . . . Would he be lonely up there?

She tried to imagine some sort of heaven where Nanny T would still be in her cottage, and where she and Maxie would be going hand in hand up the narrow cobbled path between the giant sunflowers. Nanny T would be at the door with her blue apron on, and a big bath towel, and she would say, "Maxie! Come you on in!" Then Meg would let go of his hand and Maxie, drowned Maxie, would go running up the path right into her arms, and she would dry his dripping hair, and take him inside, and shut the door . . . And Meg . . .? Meg would still be outside, standing alone on the path between the heavy sunflowers, hearing the bees buzzing, staring at the closed door . . .

She opened her eyes and realized, kneeling desolate amongst the reeds, that even with Maxie dead she was still jealous of him. Even in the heaven she had invented for him there was no room for her. He was dead. And it was her fault. There could never be any sort of heaven for her.

She sobbed with her mouth open, eyes and nose running, abandoning herself to total misery.

And then because nature is sometimes kind, she slept.

It was evening when Meg woke, and the wind had dropped.

She lay, stiff and shivering, under the grey sky, her eyes sticky with tears, wondering whether she had not just woken from a long bad dream. But if so, what was she doing down here at the beach, all on her own, in the fading light? Her mother had not come, in her padded blue dressing gown, to shake her gently and say "Wake up, darling, you've been having a nightmare." If only she had!

She struggled to her feet, remembering. She must get back quickly, and tell someone. But who? The policeman, the boatman, anyone . . . She stumbled down to the creek. The tide had run out at last. She waded through the narrow stream and on to the flat bed of the creek, and across to the marsh. Ahead of her as she ran she saw the first lights turned on in the village.

Was it absolutely certain Maxie was drowned? Surely it was just possible he might have crossed the creek in time. (Without waiting for her?) And gone back home. (Without Pokey?) Surely there must be something, just something, that would make it all come right.

First she must get home. She would know then. If he *had* got across, that was where he would be, waiting for her. But the key, she had got the key! He would not even be able to get in.

It was not the first time he had been lost, after all. She remembered the occasions in detail, comforting herself as she ran. That time last summer, for instance—Maxie sitting on the field gate by the farm, saying in his silly surprised way, "I only came to see the cows milked. Why're you looking so cross and funny? Your eyes'll fall out." He had said that to Mummy, and she'd been searching for him for hours.

And that other time, staying with Granny at Canford Cliffs, when they'd all gone plodding full speed back up the hill to where they'd last seen him. And there he'd sat by the side of the road, making a pattern of rowan berries on the pavement, quite unconcerned. No one had scolded him as far as she remembered, and she had been annoyed. He had spoilt their afternoon. "It would have served you right if we'd left you," she had told him later. "What would you have done then?" But he had only said, "I thought if you didn't come back I'd knock at the door of a house and ask for a drink."

That was so like him—to wait to be found, and confidently expect to be looked after.

It was almost dusk when she turned up the lane to the cottage. She had run faster than she ever remembered to get past the private road corner while there was still a little light. Now, exhausted and shaking, she tottered up to the front door. He was not there. Nor was he in the garden. Nor in the little yard round the back.

Her hands trembled so much she had difficulty getting the key into the lock. She leaned her whole weight against the door, and nearly fell in when at last the lock turned. It was dark inside. She switched on the light, and called. There was no answer.

Disappointment hit her like a blow in the stomach. Her legs gave way and she sat down on the bottom stair.

Now what was she to do?

Meg sat with her head in her hands, thinking. What ought she to do? Where ought she to go?

She got up and went into the kitchen. Was it only today they had all been here, having breakfast? Mummy and Hannah talking about a possible emergency—heavens above!—and Maxie worrying about his kite. Oh, Maxie! Could it really have been only this morning? If only they were all here now, even Hannah on her own. But there was nothing for it, she knew what she must do. It was too far to go all the way back to the village. It would soon be dark, and she had no torch. Anyway there was a hurry. She had lost too much time already. If only her knees would stop trembling!

She went over to the fridge and took a long drink of

milk out of the bottle. Milk was supposed to make you strong, people said. She needed to be strong now.

She went to the front door and opened it. After the brightness of the kitchen it seemed darker outside. But the light from behind her lit up something she had not noticed on coming in. A long leafy branch had been laid over the lintel of the door, and something was hanging from the end of it. It looked like a tiny doll. She jumped and flicked it down and saw that it was an ordinary little pink plastic doll, tied by a thread round its neck to a branch of elderberry.

But the sight of it made her shiver suddenly. Who could have put it there? Maxie was not tall enough, even if he had been there. And it reminded her of something . . . something creepy . . . She stared at the doorstep, trying to remember. It was something Nanny T had once told her about—how when she was a child she had seen a dolly left on someone's doorstep to put an evil spell on them, and no one had dared step over it, not even grown ups.

She shuddered and flung it quickly away from her with all her strength. It landed somewhere over by the hedge, she thought, in the long grass. Then she ran down the path and out into the lane. Who but a witch would have done that? If it was not sinister and evil it was such a plain dotty thing to do. Could Mrs Jarvis have come to the cottage after all, when they were out? But why should she want to leave an evil spell over their door? Perhaps to punish them for running away so quickly when she spoke to them yesterday.

But she must not panic.

She slowed down to a steady jog-trot. It would be asking for trouble to arrive panting and frightened. She remembered what her father had always said about dogs, that if you looked frightened they would be more likely to attack you. Whatever happened she must not look frightened. Not that Mrs Jarvis would attack her exactly. It would be something more scary than that, more sinister . . . like that horrible little doll hanging from the elderberry branch. But she must not think of that. At least Maxie was out of danger, that sort of danger, now. As long as she could just phone home (how would she tell them, whatever would they say?) after that Mrs Jarvis could do what she liked. It didn't much matter what happened to her. Nothing could be worse than what had happened already.

She turned into the coast road. The tall hedges stood out black against the afterglow of the sunset. In the gaps between the branches she saw the sky grey above, shading down to green, then orange and low on the horizon, streaks of fiery red. It was fading already. Soon it would be dark.

What should she say to Mrs Jarvis when she got there? "Please may I use your phone?"—as if it were nothing special—or should she tell her what had happened and ask to phone home? But that would be telling her they were away . . . In any case, she would pretend she had not seen that thing over the door.

Ahead, against the dark clump of bushes at the corner (elderberry bushes, of course!) the finger post loomed palely white. *Private Road* . . . this was it. She drew a deep breath of fresh air and turned the corner.

Immediately she stumbled and almost fell. The lane was much darker than the road had been, and rutted, with little hummocks of grass sticking up in unexpected places. At first she could see nothing ahead of her but the straggly hedge. Then, as the track straightened out, she saw at the far end the dark mass of house, barn, and outbuildings that must be Rook Hall. Beyond it, between the trees, the last red glimmers of the sunset still glowed. It looked grim, spooky, she thought.

Something black flitted past, close to her face, darting raggedly from side to side, and her hands flew up to her head. A bat! Weren't they supposed to get caught in your hair? She stood rigid until it disappeared in the darkness, then went on up the track.

As she drew nearer, the house rose up in front of her, silhouetted against the sky, and she saw to her dismay that there were no lights in any of the windows. She had not expected that. She went through a gateway, where the gate was half off its hinges and leaning drunkenly sideways, passed an outhouse, and came to the front door. At least, she supposed it was the front door because of the pillars though a great pile of wood lay at the side of the step.

Fumbling, she found the bell and pressed it. Then she stood, quaking. Nothing happened. She pressed it again, then a third time, putting her ear against the door to hear if the bell was ringing inside. But she could hear nothing.

The trees creaked slightly and leaves rustled in the bushes by the broken gate. She spun round and stood with her back to the door, facing the possible danger. But it was nothing. She must think. This was something she had not foreseen, that Mrs Jarvis might be out.

An owl hooted suddenly, close at hand, making her

start with fear, and reminding her of all the things she had ever heard about witches. They liked darkness, they went out at night to do their evil work, they made wicked spells to harm people . . . A terrible thought struck her. That doll over the door. Had it been meant to represent Maxie? It had been hanging, and Maxie had been drowned, but it could have been part of a wicked spell to make him get drowned. She remembered suddenly how Mrs Pacey had called her 'that sea-witch woman' . . .

So it was Mrs Jarvis's fault, not hers.

But why should Mrs Jarvis want to harm him? Perhaps she hadn't. Perhaps she had made the spell too strong. No, she knew what it was! She had wanted to steal him. That was why she had always looked at him so strangely. The spell would have been to draw him towards her house in some mysterious way, just as she had imagined. It was natural Mrs Jarvis should have wanted Maxie rather than herself. People always did. It was something to do with the way he looked. And he was younger. Instead of seeing him as a fairy child (like Granny) she had seen him as a witch's child, and wanted him for herself. The thought horrified her.

The owl hooted again, horribly near, and she jumped nervously. Did Mrs Jarvis know what had happened to Maxie now? Had she gone out to look for him, to find out why her spell hadn't worked? When she knew he was drowned she was going to be very angry. She might think it was Meg's fault. She stopped short. Was she imagining all this? She didn't think so.

But whatever Mrs Jarvis was up to, whatever she thought, was not important at this minute. The immediate thing was to try and phone home. She felt herself whimpering, silently inside herself, with the sudden need to hear her mother's voice. But then she, too, would be angry . . .

Cautiously, she made her way round to the back of the house, thinking confusedly that if she could only discover where the telephone was kept, she might even break a window and climb in. Once she had it in her hand, had dialled, and got through, nothing else would matter. Not even if they were angry. She must expect that. (But hadn't she always looked after him?)

She came out between a clump of rhododendron bushes, then stopped dead. Light was glimmering faintly on the leaves of a creeper further along the house wall. There must be a lighted window along there, on the ground floor.

Stealthily she crept along by the wall until she reached the place. She stood listening, but could hear only the faint creaking of branches in a large tree close by. Then she put her hands on the sill and jumped, holding on to the stone ledge, her feet desperately scrabbling for a foothold in the wall. But there was none. She slipped slowly down until her feet landed in the soft earth again. Then she stood trembling with astonishment, excitement, and a kind of horror. Could she really believe what she had just seen? Or was she imagining it?

In those few seconds, before her hands slipped, she had seen right into the room. The light had been coming from a circle of flickering candles, and in the centre of that circle, sitting absolutely still, looking as if he had been turned to stone, was Maxie.

7

"Who's There?"

Dazed, Meg sucked her grazed fingertips and jumped again. The need to make sure helped her to stay balanced longer this time.

Maxie *was* there! She had not imagined it. He hadn't been drowned. Or had he, and was he now sitting there dead? Oh no! She rejected the thought almost before it was formed. But there was something so uncanny, so unearthly, about the way he looked. He was still sitting surrounded by candles, his profile to the window, unmoving, staring blankly into space. And he was wearing some sort of white shawl or robe draped round his shoulders.

Her hands slipped, and again she fell. Again she jumped. This time she saw Mrs Jarvis move forward out of the shadows at the back of the room, one arm held out in front of her. Meg felt, rather than saw, that she was looking at him with that same brooding, intent expression that had always frightened them, and her blood ran cold. Still Maxie did not move.

So the spell had worked! And it was true! She realized in that instant that she had never *really* believed in witches right up to that minute. She had played at believing in them. Yet she had been right all along . . . Her fingers gave way, and she dropped down into the earth in a limp, trembling heap.

So Mrs Jarvis was a witch. Not a frighten-yourself-to-death-for-fun kind of witch, but a real one. And it *had* been a spell to draw him into her house, just as she'd suspected. (No wonder she hadn't opened the door!) She'd probably started working on it at Rook Hall days ago. That would be why he'd suddenly wanted to go past her lane yesterday—and then she'd said *why don't you let him choose the way* when Meg had tried to make him go the other way, knowing of course that he would choose the way *she* wanted if left to himself. Meg felt a certain pride to think she must have sensed the spell even then.

It was cold sitting on the ground, and wet too; the dew had started to settle. Over the far end of the house the dead branch of an oak tree hung, dark against the pale sky, like a large black claw. Meg shivered.

How had the spell actually worked? Spells were something younger children believed in usually. Yet it was a useful word to use for things you couldn't explain ordinarily. (Like 'isolated.' You might well need to be isolated because of an evil influence, a bad magic or something.) Huddled under the window, she tried to work out how Mrs Jarvis could actually have got hold of Maxie. By some sort of influence, she supposed, which might have worked in a quite ordinary-seeming way. He would have decided not to go to Nanny T's after all, but to go home, feeling drawn to go the way past her little lane—it was the shortest way, after all—and she would have been there waiting for him, laughing quietly, like she was yesterday.

What then? Surely he would have been scared to go all the way with her down that horrible dark little lane. She had probably had to drag him there in the end, screaming all the way. But no one would have heard because it was so far away from other houses.

Who would hear now if she should scream? No one but Mrs Jarvis. Maxie looked past hearing anything. She had bewitched him, put a spell on him, or hypnotised him or something—probably to stop him screaming—and that was why he was sitting there now, looking like a stone statue. Oh, horrible!

Once more she jumped, and clung to the sill. Nothing had changed. Then, as she stared, she saw Maxie blink. Just once. No other part of him moved, but it was enough. He was not petrified—yet.

She let go, fell on her knees, scrambled up again and hobbled, stiff with fear, round to the front of the house.

The solid door faced her. Not a chink of light showed under it, nor round the edges. In the pitchy darkness she stumbled over an iron boot scraper and hurt her ankle. There must be a knocker. She reached up and felt for it. There was one, but it was too rusted to lift.

How was she to get in? She would smash the door down if she had to! Maxie must be rescued whatever happened.

She stepped backwards to see if there was now any light showing in the window above, and fell over the pile of logs.

A log, that was the thing! She seized one and crashed it against the door. After the first blow she listened. She had disturbed only a bird that was sleeping in the creeper above, otherwise there was silence. Absolute silence. That blow must have rung through the whole house. Even if Mrs Jarvis was stone deaf she would have heard it.

Supposing she didn't answer! But she would—she must! What would happen then? If only there was someone else here, someone really strong, like her father! She beat on the door again, a rain of blows, then paused to listen. It occurred to her that she could always pretend she had someone with her.

She banged again, and heard sounds inside. Footsteps, and a clanking sound, as though a can had been knocked over, followed by an annoyed exclamation.

She raised her voice and shouted to the bushes by the gate: "I shan't be a minute! Wait for me!" But her voice sounded quavery and foolish in the silence. She tried again. "Wait for me! I won't be a minute!" and even tried to follow it up with a deep growl of "All right," but that sounded even more foolish.

Then she heard the rattle of bolts being drawn back inside. A chain was unlatched, and with creaks and groans the door opened.

Mrs Jarvis stood there, holding a candle in a bottle over her head. She leaned forward, hardly seeming to see Meg, and said in her deep husky voice, "Who's there?"

"Me," said Meg, her teeth chattering.

Mrs Jarvis looked down at her. By the light of the candle her face looked older, with long lines down each side of her mouth, and deep, hooded eyes.

"Who else?" she demanded. Meg hesitated. "Who were you talking to just now? Is someone else there?"

Meg waved a hand shakily towards the bushes. Mrs Jarvis raised her voice and shouted into the night.

"Hello! Hello there! Do you mind coming forward where I can see you?" The candlelight wavered over the bushes. No one came out. Meg gave up.

"There isn't anyone there," she said. She took a deep breath and braced herself. "I want to know what you've done to my little brother. I—you've got to stop it—You've got to undo it—*Now!*"

Then, suddenly, with a kind of desperate courage—expecting to be turned to stone herself at any minute—she was attacking Mrs Jarvis, beating at her with her fists, kicking, scratching, even biting her hand when it came out to restrain her. And she was screaming, "You've stolen him! You're wicked, *you're wicked*! Give him back, or I'll kill you!"

The next thing Meg knew was that she had been dragged into the house, still kicking and screaming, and was being half carried, half pulled, down a long dark stone passage.

Then she did not even know that.

8

Candles in Bottles

Meg was propped up on a low divan with a cushion behind her head. The circle of candles flickered brightly over by the window, but Maxie was no longer there. Her head ached, a big bump seemed to be coming up on her forehead. She must have bumped it on that dungeon wall.

But she was not in a dungeon now. She was in a strange room lit only by candlelight. The candles were all stuck in long dark bottles, some of them with wax running all the way down their sides, making peculiar bobbly shapes. She heard movements behind her, then Maxie's voice saying in a loud whisper:

"What happened?"

"I think she bumped her head, that's all. I'm just getting her something."

Meg sat up and looked round. They were over in the far corner of the room. Mrs Jarvis was bending over a small stove. Maxie saw her and came running across on tiptoe, his strange white garment trailing behind him. He was smiling happily.

"What happened?" he asked. "Did you bump your head? You made an awful lot of noise."

"I think something frightened her as well," said Mrs

Jarvis, coming over with a mug in her hand. She looked down at Meg with a wry smile. "Well, that was a fine how-d'you-do, I must say. All right now?"

Maxie leaned anxiously towards Meg. "Did you see the ghost, Meg, the spurious ghost? Was that it?"

Mrs Jarvis laughed, suddenly and loudly. "Might well be," she said. "Anything's possible in this place!" She handed the mug to Meg. "Now drink that. You'll feel better."

Meg looked at it suspiciously. "What is it?"

"Hot lemon mainly."

"What else?"

"Glucose."

Meg looked doubly suspicious. "What's glucose?"

"Same as sugar, more or less."

Meg brooded over this reply, then handed the mug back. "No, thank you. I'd rather not."

"Oh my God, child! What d'you think I'm trying to do? Poison you, or put a spell on you, or what?" Meg, who had been thinking just that, was taken aback. Mrs Jarvis laughed again, but roughly as if she was annoyed. She picked a wine glass off the table behind her, poured some of the liquid into it and drank it down in one gulp.

"Now—when I don't drop down dead or turn into a toad, perhaps you'll drink the rest?" She gave a grim little smile and shook her head. "Not my idea of a drink either," she said, "but it'll do you good."

Meg drank it, and was relieved to find she did feel better. She needed to. She was still deeply suspicious of Mrs Jarvis. She would need all her strength. She glowered at her from under her eyelashes, rubbing the bump on her head.

"Does it hurt?" said Mrs Jarvis. "It was your own fault, you know."

"No, it wasn't," said Meg rudely. "It was you, dragging me through that dungeon."

"Dungeon?" Mrs Jarvis lifted her black eyebrows. "You mean the passage?"

"Well, it was dark—and all stone—" Meg began to feel slightly silly. (Had it only been a passage? It had felt like a dungeon.)

"I admit it's rather a slum, but I hadn't thought of it as a dungeon," said Mrs Jarvis, and murmured something about putting down some red carpet if she had known Meg was coming. (Why *not* anyway, thought Meg? You don't wait till people come before putting carpets down.) But there was a lot more needed explaining yet.

"It was your fault," she said angrily, though she was quaking inside, "making him come here. He never would have on his own." She half closed her eyes in what she hoped was a threatening look. "I know now what you meant yesterday, when you said about letting him choose the way. You were planning to get him here. You've been wanting to a long while. That's why I wouldn't let him. He was always quite safe with me."

Mrs Jarvis lifted one eyebrow. "Quite safe? Even today?"

"Yes, of course. Until you interfered. You should have left him alone."

"What a nasty little girl you are," said Mrs Jarvis.

Meg began to think she might be getting the upper hand.

"What were you doing to him when I came?" she asked in an accusing voice.

Mrs Jarvis stared. "Doing to him?"

"Yes. Don't pretend you don't know. I saw you, through the window."

"Heavens above, child!" Mrs Jarvis glanced towards the window. "If you could climb that high, you must know what I was doing. Making a sketch of him. Do you mind?" Meg glowered. "I didn't make him sit for hours, if that's what you mean. About five minutes, was it?" She turned to Maxie, who had been listening, wide-eyed, and now nodded his head, grinning.

"She's going to make a picture of me, Meg. A real one!"

Meg was silent, taking this in. She was inclined to think it was true. It did look like an easel standing by the window. After all, there was no reason why a witch should not paint. But she was still suspicious.

"Then what are the candles for?" she demanded.

Mrs Jarvis got up and helped herself to a drink from a tall dark bottle.

"To make light," she said calmly.

Maxie laughed. Meg was angry now. How dare Mrs Jarvis make fun of her in front of Maxie?

"You should have a proper light," she said.

"I prefer candlelight," said Mrs Jarvis, drawing herself up.

"Well, I don't," said Meg. "At least, not here."

"Then we must agree to disagree," said Mrs Jarvis frostily.

Meg looked at Maxie. He seemed happy enough. Mrs Jarvis couldn't have been badly ill-treating him. She almost wished she had. She would have felt in a stronger position then. But she still did not trust her.

"Why didn't you answer the door?" she demanded. "When I rang?"

"Oh, you rang! I'm sorry. No wonder you were bashing the door down. But I didn't know you were coming."

"I rang three times," said Meg sternly.

Mrs Jarvis stood up, looking taller than ever. "The door bell doesn't ring," she said, "for the same reason that I have no electric light. Because the electricity has been cut off."

Meg looked as if she did not quite believe this, and mumbled that she thought Mrs Jarvis had lights on in her house all night. Mrs Jarvis looked at her with a sort of quiet amazement.

"So I did," she said. "Quite often, before they cut it off. I prefer staying up late. I've always been a night bird."

"Like a owl?" said Maxie. "Who-oo, who-o-o!"

"That's right." Mrs Jarvis grinned at him. But Meg felt as if cold water had begun trickling down her back.

"Why?" she said.

Mrs Jarvis frowned impatiently, her eyebrows looking blacker than ever.

"Why what? Why did they cut it off? I suppose because they've got the extraordinary idea that I owe them some money."

Maxie looked concerned. "And don't you?"

"I'm quite sure I do." She turned to Meg who was confused because that was not what she had meant. She had only been trying to discover whether Mrs Jarvis would admit to being a witch.

"Do we have to go into this sort of thing," said Mrs Jarvis. "I feel as if I'm in the witness box." She looked tired, half amused, half angry. "Any more questions?"

"Yes," said Meg bravely, clenching her fists. "I want to know how you got hold of Maxie." Mrs Jarvis's black eyebrows went right up. She looked astonished. Then her face relaxed, and she let out a sudden roar of laughter.

"How I got hold of him! Much the same way as I got hold of you, young woman. With both arms, pulling and tugging for dear life. But he struggled manfully, I must say."

Maxie was laughing too. "Yes, but you won!" His eyes clouded over suddenly, and he turned to Meg. "But I lost Pokey. We've got to find him tomorrow. I think I dropped him when we were fighting."

"*We* weren't fighting," said Meg, looking virtuous and defensive at the same time.

Maxie laughed again. "Not *you*," he said, as though he would have scorned to fight anyone so puny. "Her."

"Where were you fighting?" said Meg, now hopelessly confused.

"In the water. That's why I'm wearing this. I got soaked." He looked at Mrs Jarvis with a guilty giggle. "Her too. She was in the boat and I didn't want to get in."

Meg was still confused and far from satisfied. She let her eyes wander round the room, partly to gain time, partly to avoid Mrs Jarvis's gaze. Why did the place look so odd, so weird? All those candles in bottles, for one thing, and the shadows they made on everything. Huge paintings, that made no sense to her, hung on the walls—paintings of people with enormous bodies and tiny heads, or only one eye, or just strange shapes.

(Whatever sort of picture would she make of Maxie!)

The furniture was mostly large and dark and had an accidental look about it, as though no one had ever thought of arranging it. A large round table at Mrs Jarvis's elbow appeared to be covered with things—jars with paintbrushes in, papers, a type-writer, more bottles, packets of candles, and what looked like a frying pan with a spoon in it. Never had she seen such an untidy room.

She caught Mrs Jarvis's eye and looked down at the floor. That too was littered, with crumbs and paper bags.

"Well?" said Mrs Jarvis.

"I don't know what you've both been talking about," said Meg sulkily.

Mrs Jarvis pulled forward a low chair with a broken back, and sat down on it opposite Meg, with her knees apart. Under her long skirt, splashed with mud, Meg saw the outsize wellington boots, also splashed with mud.

"It's my turn to ask questions now," said Mrs Jarvis firmly. "What happened?"

"When?" said Meg, slightly startled. (What hadn't happened!)

"Don't fob me off." Mrs Jarvis jerked her head impatiently. "Start at the beginning. How come you left your little brother alone on the beach? Weren't you supposed to be looking after him?"

"Yes, but he ran away."

"I didn't!" said Maxie. "Only once, at the be-ginning."

"Where were you, then?" said Meg.

"In a hole."

"What does he mean?" said Mrs Jarvis.

"A hollow, in the sandhills. But he wasn't. I looked and looked." She turned angrily on Maxie. "Why didn't you come out? You must have heard me calling you."

He shook his head. "I didn't. I was hiding at first, but after that I think I went to sleep. When I woke up, you'd gone."

Mrs Jarvis looked at Meg. There was a long silence.

"I did look," said Meg at last. "Then, when I couldn't find him I thought perhaps he'd gone over to Nettleton marsh, so I ran over there, but it was all misty and I couldn't see him. Then I thought he must be on the island after all, so I went back—I had a little rest first—and when I got to the creek the tide was beginning to come in, so I rushed over to the island, but he still wasn't there. I waited on the sea side after that. I thought he might have gone along the beach."

"Ah." Mrs Jarvis nodded her head. "That must be how we missed you. Now I'll tell you what happened to us."

She had gone for a row, she said, down the creek to the island, and seen Maxie standing all alone by the water, obviously fed up. (How anyone could have just left him there she could not imagine.) The tide was coming in fast and it was too deep to paddle across, so she'd offered him a lift, but he'd refused. Then she'd asked him where his parents were, and he'd said, gone away; where his sister was, he didn't know. And someone called Hannah, she gathered, had gone away too. Meg nodded. Mrs Jarvis couldn't leave him there alone, so she'd forced him into the boat, and he'd fought all the way, splashing and kicking.

"It had water in," said Maxie. "I thought you were going to sink me."

Mrs Jarvis nodded seriously and agreed that it was a leaky old tub. She'd bought it with the house, she said, just as it was, and it had served her well enough though it hadn't had a lick of paint in years from the look of it. "But it never expected to have people *fighting* in it," she said.

Here Maxie laughed, as if it had all been a great joke, and Mrs Jarvis said: "Fetch my pipe from next door, will you, boy-o? I'm ready for a puff."

Meg looked up quickly—was she joking?—but Mrs Jarvis was not smiling. When Maxie had gone, she said sternly, "That kid was frightened out of his wits. Why?"

There seemed no answer to this, so Meg said nothing.

Mrs Jarvis went on. Maxie had sat shuddering in the boat, she said, all the way back as if he was being kidnapped or something. And it had been even worse getting him into the house (wasn't anybody *ever* kind to him?) He'd clung on to the gatepost as if he was going to be imprisoned, or swallowed alive. However, he had cheered up after tea, and they'd gone round to the cottage, but found no one there.

"What I want to know," she said, leaning right forward and speaking slowly and deliberately, "is where *you* were? Where have you been all this time?"

Meg pressed herself back against the wall. Her eyes clouded, and she became quite closed up in herself.

"On the island," she mumbled at last, her lips barely moving.

"No, after that. When the tide came up." Meg

nodded silently. "You don't mean you got stuck there! But what about Maxie, weren't you bothered?"

Meg looked sulky, not trusting herself to speak.

"What did you imagine had happened to him?"

"I thought he'd got drowned," said Meg, and burst into tears.

9

Mussels-and-Mash

Everything seemed to get better after that.

Mrs Jarvis got up and said, "Oh you poor kid! I'd got you all wrong. I'm sorry. Stop snivelling, there's a good girl. You make me feel a brute." Then she looked vaguely round and said, "My God, you must be starving!"

Maxie came running in with the pipe in his hand—a man's pipe—and Meg stared at it through her tears. "Yes, that's mine," said Mrs Jarvis, taking it from him, "but I'll save it for now."

Maxie looked at Meg and said: "Why are you crying?" And Mrs Jarvis said: "She isn't now. She's stopped. She's hungry, poor thing. D'you know she's had no tea?"

"Golly!" said Maxie in a shocked voice. "I had a huge one."

"Can't be helped," said Mrs Jarvis. "She's missed it." She picked up one of the paper bags that littered the floor and peered hopefully inside, but it was empty. She looked thoughtful. "We'll have to have supper instead."

She began to clear one side of the table. Food was important, she said. It was always important to eat.

People forgot that sometimes. She moved the type-writer to the floor, pushed the papers and jars aside, and looked with surprise at the frying pan. She investigated it carefully, turning over the contents with the spoon, then said:

"Well I'm blowed, that was my last night's supper. No wonder I felt a bit peckish this morning!" She laughed uproariously, then was suddenly solemn again.

"Food," she said, and stood wrapped in thought.

Half an hour later they were all sitting down to the oddest meal Meg had ever seen. All sorts of things were piled together on one large tray in the centre of the table. Each of them had a plate, and that was that.

"Take what you like the look of, when you like, and how you like," said Mrs Jarvis. "Spoons on the tray."

Maxie did not seem at all surprised and tucked in happily to fried bread spread with jam, with bacon on top, eating with his fingers. To Meg it seemed a strange mixture, as did the slice of cheese, also spread with jam, that Mrs Jarvis was nibbling. But it did look interest-ing. She chose the same as Maxie and was surprised how good it tasted. To drink they had evaporated milk out of a tin, poured into tea with lots of sugar. There were also slices of coarse brown bread and butter, piled high with raisins, some rather wrinkled looking apples, and a pie-dish full of something which Mrs Jarvis called mussels-and-mash.

"Mussels?" said Maxie. "That's what that notice is about."

Mrs Jarvis looked blank. Meg explained. "There's a notice on the staithe saying all mussels are private property."

Mrs Jarvis laughed. "I never go on the staithe," she

said. "But seagulls can't read. Count me a seagull. They love 'em." Meg shivered suddenly. "It's nicer than it looks," said Mrs Jarvis, "try some."

"It isn't that," said Meg. "It reminded me of the seagulls on the island, the way they were screaming when I was alone down there. I thought they were screaming at me."

"Forget it," said Mrs Jarvis. "They probably mistook you for a herring." She patted Meg's knee under the table. Meg glanced down and saw long red scratches and a deep ring of toothmarks on the back of Mrs Jarvis's hand. She looked away again quickly. Mrs Jarvis drew her hand back.

"What were we talking about?" she said.

"Going on the staithe," said Maxie. "Why don't you?"

Meg looked up, suddenly remembering about her being isolated.

"No need," said Mrs Jarvis with a shrug. "I leave it to the sailing types once the holidays start. Anyway I keep my boat nearer home." She explained that the fields at the back of Rook Hall ran down to the creek, lower down than the staithe, so she only had to pull her dinghy up on to the bank below the dyke, and walk back across the fields.

"I miss everybody that way," she said, as if the idea pleased her.

"Then you are isolated?" Meg asked cautiously.

"Only from the village, I suppose. But that suits me. Too much chin-wagging there."

"What's that?" said Maxie.

"Gossiping, silly talk. I don't go there unless I must."

"But you are allowed to if you *want* to?" Meg persisted.

"Well, of course. It's a free country!" Mrs Jarvis looked as if she might be going to laugh, then changed her mind.

"But when I had spots—" Maxie began.

"He had to keep away from people then," Meg interrupted. "But that was different, wasn't it? I mean you aren't really isolated if you're allowed to, are you?"

"No," said Mrs Jarvis with a funny sideways smile, she was not as dangerous as all that. But East Anglia was a funny place; if you were a stranger and did things differently from other people, they thought there was something funny about you. They were probably quite right, but not *that* sort of funny.

"What sort of funny?" said Maxie.

She brushed the question aside and poured herself another drink from the tall dark bottle.

"My house is isolated because I prefer it that way," she said, in the same voice as she had said earlier that she preferred candlelight. "But don't let's talk about *them* any more. They make me tired."

"I'm a bit tired too," said Maxie in a bright conversational tone. "But this is such a nice supper I expect it'll wake me up again." (Somehow Maxie was always able to make pleasant, polite remarks like that.)

Supper over, Mrs Jarvis leaned back and lit her pipe. Blue smoke curled around the room. Maxie's eyelids drooped—in spite of the nice supper, or perhaps because of it. Now that there seemed so little to fear after all, Meg found her own eyelids growing heavy. But they must go home. She glanced at the window. It was quite dark outside. Once more the owl hooted dismally up in the tree. There was no point in putting it off. Perhaps Mrs Jarvis would offer to go part of the way back with them. (How strange to find herself thinking that!) She pushed back her chair.

"I think we'd better go now."

Mrs Jarvis looked mildly surprised. "Go where?"

"Home."

Mrs Jarvis shook her head. "No, I don't think so." She looked at Meg with her intent dark gaze. "Tell me, do your parents often leave you alone?"

"No, never! It's never happened before, and it was a mistake this time." And gradually, with Maxie chipping in, she told her about Hannah, and her letter, and the wedding; and before long Mrs Jarvis knew all about their parents' trip to London, and what a rush it had all been, getting Hannah off and everything.

"And all this happened today?" said Mrs Jarvis. "No wonder you were both falling asleep on the beach!"

"We'd walked a terrible long way as well," said Maxie earnestly. "Miles and miles, didn't we, Meg? We went the long way round to the creek, right through the village."

"Oh? Why did you do that?"

"Because—" Maxie stopped short, caught Meg's eye, then clapped his hand over his mouth and sniggered. Meg stretched out her foot as far as it would go under the table, but he was too far away to kick.

"Because what?" said Mrs Jarvis.

Maxie began to giggle foolishly, glancing sideways at Meg, then gazing up at the ceiling as if searching for the answer there. Meg recognized the gleam in his eye and held her breath.

"Because we had to," he said at last. "For a secret reason."

"Oh," said Mrs Jarvis. "And when will they be coming back?"

"Tomorrow," said Meg, breathing freely again. "Some time after tea. At least, Mummy will." She caught Maxie looking at her with an expression half guilty, half laughing, and frowned fiercely. He looked away.

"Then you'd better stay here," said Mrs Jarvis. "If they're not here they can't miss you." She got up and went across to the divan. "Come and sit here. It's more comfortable."

Maxie followed her with little yelps of delight, and climbed up beside her, jumping up and down on the divan till the springs creaked. He was obviously excited at the thought of staying the night, and it annoyed Meg to see how perfectly at home he was already in this strange place. (But of course, as usual, he had got there first.) She stood uncertainly by the table, staring down at the empty plates.

"Don't look at those," said Mrs Jarvis, patting the place beside her. "Time enough to think of washing up next time we're hungry."

Meg went over and sat down gingerly. She was still a little frightened of Mrs Jarvis, and she was worried at the way Maxie was behaving. In this silly mood he might say anything. But with Mrs Jarvis between them it was difficult to keep any control over him. She set her face in a savage glare and turned her head sideways, ready to catch his eye next time he bounced into view. But it was Mrs Jarvis who looked round first. She caught the full force of the glare, in close-up, and Meg hardly knew whether to feel frightened or foolish.

Mrs Jarvis stared at her thoughtfully.

"Why do you have to run so fast past the end of my lane?" she asked suddenly.

Maxie giggled. Meg was silent, wondering how often Mrs Jarvis might have seen her dragging him along, and scolding him.

"And why was he so frightened?"

Meg jumped. "When?"

"Yesterday. When you passed. I was watching a wren in the hedge—it's wonderful how much birds will let you see if you only keep still enough. But I wondered what made him so frightened?"

Maxie sprawled, chuckling, on the divan, waving his legs in the air.

"You did!" he said.

"Me?"

"Yes, you were going to put a spell on us!"

"Was I indeed?"

"Yes, and you were going to put me in a cage and fat me up to eat!" He was really enjoying himself now, rolling from side to side on the divan, giggling idiotically.

"*Was* I?" said Mrs Jarvis.

"Yes—you often are—" said Maxie, and in his delight rolled clean off the end of the divan.

"Dear me!" said Mrs Jarvis, smiling.

Oh please let that stop him, thought Meg. But it didn't. He scrambled up again, choking with laughter, and carried straight on.

"Yes—you often are, if I'm dawgling—or won't hurry or something—And you eat spiders—and chase children—and have a horrible big black cat with fierce eyes—and you make wicked, creepy spells—and—and—"

It was useless for Meg to try and stop him. He was now staring round the room, his eyes full of laughter tears, giggling helplessly as he tried to remember further inventions of her own. She hated him—hated him, but there was nothing she could do about it. She stared down at her lap, waiting for the blow to fall.

Mrs Jarvis turned round.

"You abominable creature," she said, in a perfectly friendly voice, and stroked Meg's hair.

Surprised, muddled, relieved, and suddenly very tired, Meg felt tears smarting behind her eyelids.

"Bed," said Mrs Jarvis, springing up. "Now where shall we put you?"

She prowled about the room, pushing chairs around, pulling a shawl off a screen, taking down coats from the back of the door, collecting cushions together, and in a few minutes had it all worked out. Maxie was to sleep in the two biggest armchairs, pulled together. Meg was to have the divan.

"Isn't it your bed?" said Meg gruffly.

"Only when I forget to go upstairs, and fall asleep here by mistake," said Mrs Jarvis. "Tonight I shall go to bed properly like a lady."

She had no pyjamas small enough, she said, so they would have to go to bed as they were, but they could take off their top layers if they liked, and their shoes. Maxie already had, and having arrived with no shoes, was ready as he stood. He could sleep in the robe. Meg took off her sandshoes, jersey, and jeans and left it at that.

If they were mad about hygiene, they could wash their hands at the sink in the scullery, Mrs Jarvis said, but they would find the water cold. She would leave a light—another candle in a bottle—on the window sill in the lavatory at the end of the passage. "And mind you don't fall over the oil cans as you go. I always do."

Perhaps on second thoughts, to save the clatter, she wouldn't give them any more to drink tonight, but they could have apples beside them in bed. "In case you wake up thirsty," she said. "You may have to spit out the skins, but they're good and sweet inside and no maggots."

It was all rather exciting, it was so different from home. If Meg had not still been cross with Maxie she would have enjoyed sharing it with him. As it was, she pretended not to hear when he sidled up to her at intervals with little whispered remarks, such as "It's nice here, isn't it? I think it's cosy," and "Do you wish you had the chairs?" And once, when they met in the passage outside the lavatory, and he said, suddenly scared in the gloom: "But what about the ghost, Meg, will it be all right?" she ran past him, back into the lighted room without a word.

After all, he didn't need her, she told herself. He had Mrs Jarvis now. Let him ask her.

When the chairs had been pushed together, endways on, and Mrs Jarvis had collected together all the bed covers she could think of, she turned to Maxie. He had grown quiet and thoughtful during the last few minutes.

"Bed for you," she said, and lifted him up over the arms of the chairs, down on to the seats inside, and tucked him up under a pile of rugs with a duffelcoat on top.

"How's that?"

"Why don't you have any bedrooms?" he asked quietly. Meg pricked up her ears. She had been wondering the same thing but had not liked to ask.

"I have," said Mrs Jarvis, "but I don't use them. They're dark, and cold, and full of cobwebs."

"Oh," said Maxie; then, in an awed whisper loud enough to be heard by anyone not stone deaf, "Is that where the spurious ghost's going to be?"

Mrs Jarvis laughed her sudden loud laugh.

"Bless you, boy! Wherever did you hear that?"

"Where did I, Meg?"

Meg gave up. "I heard someone say there was going to be a spurious ghost here soon," she said in a small voice. "But I don't suppose there is."

Mrs Jarvis laughed again. " 'Someone' sounds like a sensible person," she said. "Do you know what spurious means? It means imitation, not real. That's all."

"So a spurious ghost couldn't be a real one?"

"No, of course not. Whoever said that, meant it would be just another silly thing made up by silly people who haven't got enough to think about." She looked momentarily annoyed.

"Daddy said it," said Meg with pride.

"Good for him," said Mrs Jarvis briskly. "Now, are you ready to be folded up too?"

Meg laughed, and lay down. She, too, had been faintly worried about the ghost. Mrs Jarvis spread a blanket over her, then a huge heavy curtain, laying the end with the rings over her feet. On top of that went a

shabby Burberry, then a thick tablecloth with a bobble
fringe which she tucked in all round.

"Now lights," said Mrs Jarvis, straightening her
back. She went over to the table, picked up the bottle
she had been pouring her drinks from all the evening,
and held it up to the light. They watched, fascinated, as
she tipped it up, swallowed the last few mouthfuls,
then took another candle from a packet on the table and
pressed it down into the neck of the bottle.

"Now you've got another candlestick!" said Maxie
fatuously.

She turned round with a grin. "So I have!"

"But you've got quite a lot already," he remarked.

She looked solemn. "Yes. More than enough probably."

She turned away, lit the candle, and put it high on
top of the bookshelf.

"That's in case you wake up in the night and wonder
where you are," she said. "There's only one rule,
you're not to touch it. Promise?" They promised. She
glanced towards the circle of candles now guttering
low by the window. "That lot will soon be finished,"
she said. "I'll leave them to find their own way out."

Outside in the darkness the owl hooted again.

"Whooo, whooo!" said Maxie.

"Shut up," said Meg.

Mrs Jarvis peered down at Maxie over the chair
back.

"Are you all right down there? It's a funny sort of
bed, I know. But at least you can't roll off it."

"It's nicer than a bed. It's like a boat. I could climb
out if I wanted to."

"No you couldn't," Meg called across the room.

"Yes, I could."

"Do it then."

"No, it'd untuck my boat."

"I'll tuck you up tighter before you try," said Mrs Jarvis. She bent over him.

"What about our teeth?" said Maxie.

She looked concerned. "Need sharpening, do they? I'm sure Meg's don't." He crowed with delight, but Meg went hot in her corner, remembering.

"You smell like Christmas," said Maxie, giggling.

"Go to sleep," said Meg. "*And shut up.*" Mrs Jarvis laughed and tucked him up for the last time.

"I *could* climb out," said Maxie, his voice coming up muffled from under the pile of coverings, "but now I don't want to."

"Good night, then," said Mrs Jarvis.

She came over to Meg. "Okay?" she asked in a low voice.

Meg looked up at her over the edge of the bobble-fringed tablecloth. How tall and dark she looked, compared with their mother! "Yes—thank you," she whispered.

Mrs Jarvis sat down on the end of the divan.

"Poor little frog," she said suddenly—quietly, as if she had been thinking.

Meg jumped. Could she know about the frog! But how? Maxie would never have told her. She stared up at her with sudden suspicion.

"Well, he is, isn't he?" Mrs Jarvis murmured. "Trying to make himself feel bigger than he is."

"Oh, him—yes."

Mrs Jarvis put out a hand. "What is it? What's on your mind? Don't you feel safe here yet?"

Meg nodded. She did feel safe—that was the funny thing about it. And there was nothing on her mind now, apart from 'it,' of course, but that was ordinary, nothing special to do with now, and nothing whatever to do with Mrs Jarvis.

"Yes, I think I like it here," she said. For a moment she felt like adding that she thought she liked Mrs Jarvis too—being still surprised at the discovery—but that would have been difficult to say. Instead she looked down at the rough, bitten hand, where the ring of toothmarks still glowed dark red.

"Will it always show?"

"Heavens no! It's not tattooed in."

"I'm glad. I'm sorry."

It was nothing to worry about, Mrs Jarvis said. In another day or two no one would ever know Meg had been there. There was silence for a moment while she looked at Meg thoughtfully.

"Who told you I was a witch?"

Meg jumped again. "Nobody. I—I just thought it. At least—" she began to flounder— "I mean I made it up—mostly. To frighten Maxie."

To her surprise, Mrs Jarvis looked relieved. "That's all right, then. I'm glad. I know a few people in the village do still believe in witches. If they want to make up silly stories about me, they're welcome. But not to frighten children."

"I made it up in the beginning," said Meg, "but then I did begin to think it might be true. Then I got frightened. I was sure it was true when I came tonight."

Mrs Jarvis nodded. "I didn't tumble to it at first. How did you know he was here?"

"I didn't. I came to use the phone, then when you didn't answer I looked in the window, and saw him. I was scared to death then." She giggled self consciously.

"So you came to rescue him," said Mrs Jarvis seriously. "That was very brave." She held Meg's hand for a moment, then let out one of her sudden unexpected guffaws—muted this time, because of Maxie.

"It makes me think of gooseberries," she said and rocked with silent laughter.

Meg stared. "Gooseberries?"

"Yes. I used to frighten the daylights out of my little sister, telling her she'd die horribly if she touched the gooseberries. We weren't supposed to. But I wanted first pick—because she always seemed to get the best of everything. But I said it so often, I got to believe it myself—especially after eating too many once, and getting a terrible pain—so after that neither of us dared pick them."

"Oh, what a waste!"

"Not really. My mother made them into jam." She got up, smiling. "Sleep now, love. Goodnight. And sleep tight."

"What time is it?"

Mrs Jarvis looked at her watch. "Midnight." She laughed softly. "And you're safe as houses."

"Yes." Meg smiled back at her. "Goodnight."

She watched as Mrs Jarvis wandered around the room, picking up a book, her pipe, a lighted candle from the table, and finally drifted out of the door.

The candles in the window flickered and went out, one by one. The owl hooted faintly in the distance. Leaves rustled in the tree outside the window. Warmth crept up under the heavy covers and Meg sank down into delicious comfort. Confused thoughts ran into each other . . . the milkman . . . the island, deserted, with the wind blowing . . . a bunch of poppies . . . Hannah flying over the Channel in a pink dress . . .

"Meg," said Maxie out of the darkness.

"What?"

"Did you find a dolly hanging up over the door?"

"Yes. How did you know?"

"I left it there as a present for you. *She* gave it to me. She said she found it on the beach. I didn't want to leave it on the step in case someone took it, so she tied it to a branch and hung it up for me."

"Oh."

"Was it a surprise?"

"Yes. Yes, it was."

"Goody."

"And Maxie—"

"Yes?"

"I found Pokey. He was in the water, nearly drowned. But he's all right now. I took him home to dry."

"Oh, Meg! You *are* kind. He'll love you for ever!"

10

Breakfast with a Witch

It was extraordinary waking up next morning in Mrs Jarvis's large untidy room. At least it seemed extraordinary to Meg. Maxie, when he woke later, seemed to take it all for granted. Yet here she lay, in the one place she had most dreaded to find herself, warm, relaxed, and incredibly comfortable—in spite of a broken spring in the divan—and only mildly wondering what would be happening next.

The room looked different by daylight; still dark because of the large tree outside the window, but less mysterious now the candles were burnt out. If anything it looked even untidier: furniture arranged anyhow, pictures piled up on the floor and stacked against the walls, and in the corner, around the small oil stove, a confusion of saucepans, jars, and bottles.

There were other things Meg had not noticed the night before. Overhead, from a piece of knotted string made of many smaller lengths, hung Maxie's shorts and T shirt—very muddy, very crumpled. On a shelf along the wall, stood a big brass bell, and alongside it, a large glass jar full of shells, and a curiously carved figure that looked like an Indian goddess. Two floats in their nets hung from a hook by the door, and a dabbing fork stood in a corner.

Meg raised herself on one elbow and saw last night's mugs and dishes still lying on the table. Another mug was standing on the floor beside her. Where had that come from? She had a sudden dim memory of Mrs Jarvis giving her a drink some time in the night; a warm, watery drink of evaporated milk with cocoa sprinkled on top. Then she remembered why. She had been dreaming; she was sitting under a hedge, with Maxie shivering beside her, and he was saying over and over again, "Was I a ghost, Meg? I don't want to be, don't let me be!" She had started explaining that he must be a good boy then, and do as she told him, but he had shivered away from her, like a reflection under water, and she had woken up screaming.

How awful to wake up screaming in someone else's house! She hoped Mrs Jarvis would have forgotten by now.

Mrs Jarvis apparently had. By the time she came in, dressed but with bare feet, and her hair even more tousled than usual, Meg herself had almost forgotten it. She had been encouraging Maxie in their favourite game of going round the room without touching the floor, and Maxie, who had long since discarded the white shawl (which was somewhere at the bottom of his bed) was perched ready for a leap from the sideboard, back to the big chair which was 'home.'

Mrs Jarvis exclaimed at the sight of him standing naked on the sideboard.

"He couldn't get dressed," said Meg apologetically. "We couldn't reach his clothes."

Mrs Jarvis reached them down, saying she thought

he looked excellent the way he was, but perhaps he'd better get dressed for breakfast or he might frighten the birds.

"Why the birds?" said Meg.

"Well, there won't be anyone else coming," said Mrs Jarvis.

She helped Maxie on with his clothes. They looked oddly stiff and wrinkled.

"He looks like a concertina," said Meg.

Mrs Jarvis looked at him consideringly. "Yes—or corrugated cardboard?"

"I'd rather be a concertina," said Maxie.

"So you shall, boy-o."

"Don't they need an iron?" Meg suggested tentatively.

"Ha! An iron," said Mrs Jarvis. "I'd forgotten there were such things."

"But you've got one," said Meg, pointing to the floor behind the door.

"My door-stop?" said Mrs Jarvis. "Oh, I couldn't use that! It would wonder what had come over me."

Didn't she know it was really an iron, or did she mean she didn't like ironing, Meg wondered. Perhaps she didn't know how? Looking thoughtfully at Mrs Jarvis's long patchwork skirt, she said: "I suppose it *would* be difficult to iron all those little bits separately. I mean it would take an awful long time, wouldn't it?"

"About a hundred years, I should think," said Mrs Jarvis with a casual downwards glance. "But why are we talking about such extraordinary things? Breakfast is what we must think about now."

She started to move towards the door, then changed direction midway and wandered over to the window instead, and stood staring at the canvas propped up on the easel. She walked a few steps away from it, first to one side then the other, looking at it from all angles. Absent mindedly, she picked up a paint brush, then suddenly threw it down again.

"Breakfast!" she said, as if she had only just thought of it. "Let's go and see what we can find before we forget."

They followed her into the scullery, a small dark damp-smelling place with cobwebs hanging from the corners, and a clutter of jam jars, bottles, and oil cans littering the stone floor. While Meg filled the kettle at the sink, Mrs Jarvis peered into cupboards and looked along shelves.

"Two eggs, hooray," she said. "Nearly half a loaf, and the rest of the jam we had last night."

"But what about you?"

She shook her head. "Breakfast isn't my line. I ate hugely last night, having such good company. Bread and jam'll suit me fine." She brought out a packet of oatmeal. "Or do either of you like porridge? Evaporated milk only, though." They said they would rather have eggs. "Right, let's take these in."

She touched the electric cooker with her hand in passing. "Poor thing, I try not to look at it. It hates being unemployed, and it's my fault because of the electricity." She lowered her voice. "But secretly, between ourselves, I manage just as well without it. Most people are cluttered up with too many things anyway."

This seemed an extraordinary statement to Meg, who thought she had never seen a place so cluttered up as Rook Hall. And considering they would have to wait for the kettle to boil on the little oil stove before they could even wash up last night's dishes, and then boil again before they could make the coffee or boil the eggs, she wondered whether Mrs Jarvis really did manage as well without electricity.

But, exploring the rest of the house while waiting for breakfast, she was surprised to discover how wrong she had been. There was no clutter at all. In fact, apart from a bed and a chair in the large bare room where Mrs Jarvis had evidently spent the night (her boots were still there) there was no furniture in any of the rooms. They were all empty, some dark, with shutters drawn across the windows and, as Mrs Jarvis had said, cold and full of cobwebs. The big room downstairs where she and Maxie had slept was apparently the only room in use in all that great house. Quietly, she went down the big staircase, her footsteps echoing, glad to get back to the warm familiar jumble of the room she knew.

"Well, what did you think of it?" said Mrs Jarvis squatting over the oil stove.

"It's very—tidy," said Meg, still surprised, and unsure what to say. "And very big."

Mrs Jarvis agreed that it was very big, but said she had wanted somewhere quiet, and cottages were hard to come by these days with everyone buying them up for holiday places.

"I feel sorry for these big old houses," she said, "nobody wanting them any more. I think they still dream of the days when they were grand, full of beautiful furniture and paintings, and people having parties and big family Christmases and things. Sometimes I go round turning on the lights in all the rooms, just to let

them know they're not forgotten. At least I used to."
She frowned. "I can't now. But at least I don't insult
them by camping in them. This room used to be the
kitchen so it doesn't mind so much. In fact it's made me
very welcome, don't you think?"

Meg, not knowing quite what she meant, said: "I
like it. It feels cosy."

That, said Mrs Jarvis, was what she had meant. And
she herself had made a visitor welcome not so long ago.
Had Meg discovered her guest room yet?

Meg shook her head. "I didn't go to the very top."

"Well, do," said Mrs Jarvis. "It's the left hand attic
bedroom. Hurry, though. The coffee's made."

Meg and Maxie tore up the two flights of stairs,
wondering what they might find, and opened the door
of the little attic room. But this, too, turned out to be
empty. Only a packing case stood in one corner, and
beside it on the floor, a bundle of loose straw.

"There's nothing here," said Maxie, disappointed.

Meg went over to look. There was a slight hollow in
the straw, and lying in it were two or three halves of
broken eggshells.

"Yes, there is," she said. "It's a nest, and they were
big eggs, much bigger than ordinary birds' eggs. And
look at all this mess on the floor. Isn't that a fish's tail? I
bet it was a seagull's!"

The little window was open and a sea breeze blew
into the room, rattling the catch and blowing wisps of
straw about. They looked out, the wind riffling their
hair and singing in their ears. Below them across the
field, they saw the creek, and beyond it the marsh
spreading away into the distance. It looked wild and
beautiful, and Meg felt a shiver of pleasure at the

thought of a lonely seabird flying in from the marsh to nest up here in this great empty house.

Yes, said Mrs Jarvis, when they ran downstairs again. It had been a seagull, and her mate had fed her every day, flying in through the open window, until the babies were strong enough to fly away. "I loved it," she said. "It was like having a guest house without any of the bother. That's why I keep the window open—in case they come again. A nuisance, though, when it rains, it soaks through to the next floor down. Come on, let's eat."

Thinking about that breakfast afterwards, Meg forgot that she had been a little anxious at first because Maxie kept nearly saying the wrong things, and only remembered the jolly part. But in any case, Mrs Jarvis never seemed to mind what they said.

They sat at the same round table, with the candles and papers and bottles all pushed to one side, and with the windows open on to the garden. A summer-morning smell of marsh and sea came drifting into the room.

"You like us being here, don't you?" said Maxie.

Mrs Jarvis nodded. "For today, anyway."

"Where's your daddy?"

"Dead," said Mrs Jarvis.

"He means your husband," said Meg.

"Oh, of course! Gone," said Mrs Jarvis. She was silent for a moment, then added: "I haven't got a father, or a mother, or a husband. Nor any children. I did think I might have a cat—a big black one with fierce green eyes," she grinned mischievously, "only the birds wouldn't have stood for that."

"But you aren't really a witch, are you?" said Maxie happily.

"No, boy-o. I'm not. Nothing of the sort. But if silly people like to think so, it suits me. Saves me having to dress up and go to coffee mornings, for one thing." She snorted.

"We've got a mummy *and* a daddy," said Maxie. "Would you like to come to our house?"

Mrs Jarvis considered. "Perhaps. If you were there."

Maxie glanced quickly at Meg, then back again. "What if we were in bed?"

"That would be a pity."

He nodded his head comfortably. "We'll tell them. When they know you're safe, they might let us stay up."

Meg kicked him gently under the table. He looked puzzled, then another thought struck him.

"Might you be wearing a sack? I mean you wouldn't have to dress up for our coffee, but our mummy doesn't wear sacks, ever. But I don't think it would matter," he added hastily as Meg again reached out her foot.

Mrs Jarvis laughed and said the sack was mostly for rain. No, she thought she could be trusted not to come in a sack.

They smiled and looked relieved.

"Of course," she said seriously, "if it's only my clothes they would want to see, you could carry my dress in front of you on a clothes hanger with a notice pinned on it saying this is Mrs Jarvis's best dress. I *have* got one."

They stared at her, she was looking so solemn. Then Meg burst out laughing.

"It is a proper dress," said Mrs Jarvis, "very respectable. I mostly save it for funerals, but it would be a lovely change for it to come and visit you. I think it would cheer it up no end."

"Yes," said Maxie. "Poor dress. You bring it."

"And me inside it?"

They laughed. "Yes, you inside it. Will you?"

"Perhaps," said Mrs Jarvis. "We'll see."

She tore off the outer crust of her slice of bread in one long strip and, without moving from her place at table, flung it suddenly and neatly clean over their heads through the open window.

"For the birds," she explained. "They like crust and I like crumb." She seemed surprised at their startled faces. "Should I have carried it out to them on a tray? They'd hardly expect that. That was only a starter. They'll have oatmeal next, it's better for them." She picked up the packet from beside her and they both ducked instinctively, but this time she merely emptied some on to the table. "You watch. They'll be here in a minute. But you must keep quite still."

They did, and a moment later a blackbird flopped over the window sill and landed on the table, then a thrush, then two or three sparrows, and a blue-tit; more and more, until the air was full of the sound of their wings. Meg and Maxie held their breath, sitting still as stone, and watched as the birds pecked busily, with sharp sidelong glances, scattering oatmeal in all directions.

When at last they had all flown away, Maxie let out a long sighing breath. "I think," he said solemnly, "that table's in what our mummy calls an untalkable mess."

"Unspeakable," Meg corrected.

Mrs Jarvis peered closely at the table. "Yes, it rather is. What with one thing and another, as you might say." But she seemed quite unconcerned. "Nothing a little water and a cloth won't put right," she said, and leaned back contentedly to light her pipe.

11

The Unpaid Bill

"And tomorrow we're going to Nanny T's, aren't we, Meg?"

Maxie had been telling Mrs Jarvis all about her, while she was pushing back the chairs that had been his bed, and hanging up some of the coats and covers he had slept under.

"We were going to go yesterday but I *am* glad we didn't, or we wouldn't have come here and I like being here," he said. "That makes two nice things instead of one. Aren't I lucky?" He looked thoughtfully at Mrs Jarvis. "Nanny T loves me," he announced.

"How nice for you," said Mrs Jarvis.

"Yes. And when she knows I'm coming, she makes apple dumplings and puts raisins in. But if she isn't expecting us, she gives us bread and sugar. So tomorrow we might get both."

"Oh, boy-o, are you still hungry?" Mrs Jarvis, who had been gazing at Maxie with her brooding expression, looked suddenly worried. "Go and see if there are any of those raisins left."

"Of course he isn't," said Meg quickly, but Maxie had already gone.

Mrs Jarvis stood in front of the easel and stared at her picture with half closed eyes. She looked at it for so long that Meg came up behind her and looked too. It was a queer painting, but not so dotty as the others, she thought. Queer all the same—not a bit the sort of pretty picture most people would have made of Maxie. But it did have his listening-to-nothing look; only weren't his eyes too big, or too near the top of his head or something?

"What do you think of it?" said Mrs Jarvis, turning round suddenly.

"He looks—a bit goofy," said Meg with a self conscious smirk.

"Does that please you?"

"Half. Half not. He is my brother."

"So you half love him and half hate him, I suppose." Mrs Jarvis laughed. "I don't remember even half loving my sister, but I imagine I must have."

"Where is she now?"

"In America, I believe."

"Don't you know?"

"Not for sure. And it's a bit late to find out now," said Mrs Jarvis. "I haven't seen her for over ten years. Pity in a way. But I doubt if she'd approve of me. Nor I of her, probably. We never did really hit it off."

"Why not?"

Mrs Jarvis snorted. "She was pretty and I wasn't. She was clever and I wasn't. She only had to cry and she got whatever she wanted. I never cried." She turned to Meg with her lopsided smile. "Where's that goofy little brother of yours? I'd like to start now if he'll sit for me. You know, you were right in a way last night, when you said I'd always wanted him here. I *have* always wanted to paint him. But I didn't actually *plan* to get him here. I only hoped there might be a chance some day, if ever I got to know you."

"Well, you can now," said Meg, then felt awkward because it sounded as if she were giving permission. "I mean I'll fetch him."

"What about you? Will you be happy? You might like to wander round the place. Have a look at my stables, where I keep my imaginary horses."

Meg thought she would. It was while she was in the cobbled yard, she heard knocking on the far side of the house. Someone was knocking on the front door. Should she go? She would just look and see.

It was a man. It was Mr Duffy, the milkman, the last person she would have expected to see. His round, early morning face did not go with Mrs Jarvis, she thought. There was nothing dark about Mr Duffy. With his red hair, he was like the rising sun. Besides, hadn't he said he never went to Rook Hall? "Nor you neither, I shouldn't think," she seemed to remember him saying.

He was looking very uncomfortable as he stood there, shifting his weight from one foot to the other. He rapped again, a little harder, then stared hard at the door and cleared his throat. A moment later he was looking back over his shoulder. Once he even walked away as far as the bushes by the gate, and then back again. He had a letter in his hand.

Meg felt a little awkward. Mr Duffy had clearly not approved of Mrs Jarvis, and would certainly not have expected to find her there. But, poor man, he was still waiting.

"Mr Duffy," she said, and walked towards him.

Mr Duffy gave quite a jump. There was no smile on his face as he turned to look at her.

"Mrs Jarvis doesn't use that door," she said. "There's another one round the back. But I'll fetch her, shall I?"

"I think you'd better not," he said. "I think you'd better tell me first what you're doing here."

"We stayed the night," she said, "my brother and I."

"With Mrs Jarvis?"

"Yes."

Mr Duffy looked most doubtful. "Do your mum and dad know you're here?"

"Well, no," said Meg, "they don't yet. You see, they've been in London since yesterday."

"Oh, that's how it is." Mr Duffy looked very shocked. "Then I think you'd better come back to ours right now, to my missus."

"But they'll be back tonight," said Meg. "And Mrs Jarvis has looked after us awfully well. She gave us her last two eggs for breakfast, and last night we had mussels-and-mash for supper."

Mr Duffy looked as if he was thinking they might well have been poisoned.

"She's really very kind," said Meg, and then, because she did not think she was convincing him: "I'll go and fetch her."

She ran round to the back, and then appeared again a moment later. "She's coming," she said.

Mr Duffy was shaking his head. "There's something here I don't understand," he said. "What I want to know is why, of all people, you should pick on Mrs Jarvis to stay the night with?"

Before Meg had time to answer, Mrs Jarvis came

round the corner of the house. She stopped when she saw who it was, and stood there, palette in one hand and brush in the other.

"Uh! What d'you want?" she said in a gruff voice. It was clear she was still thinking of her painting.

"To deliver you this, ma'am," Mr Duffy said, and his face went bright red.

"What is it?"

"A bill, ma'am. The gov'nor said I was to give it you in person, seeing as how you don't take no notice of any I put in your letter box."

"Well, I wouldn't know anything about that," said Mrs Jarvis, "since I never go near my letter box. Last night was the first time I've used that door for months. So you've been posting me bills, have you?"

"I'd be pleased, ma'am, if you'd settle it now." It was quite a different Mr Duffy to the one Meg had known. No smiles. No cheerful chat. He looked as if he was going to burst with anger.

"I'm sorry," said Mrs Jarvis. "I'm afraid you'll have to wait. I'm a bit tight at the moment." And then she suddenly laughed out loud. "And I don't mean what you're thinking either!"

Mr Duffy was not amused. "I didn't come here to joke," he said. "I come for the money. But now I'm here," he went on, "I've seen another little matter to set to rights. It'd be on me conscience if I didn't see to it. It's not right nor proper these two children should be in this place without the knowledge of their parents. So I'm telling you, ma'am, that, with or without your permission, I'm removing them to more suitable company, namely my wife's."

"You'd better ask them about that," said Mrs Jarvis,

flourishing her brush in the air. "That's their affair. But, tell me, Mr Duffy, this money you say I owe you," and she brought the brush down until it pointed at him, "that's a serious matter. You say the bills are in my letter box?" She turned quickly to Meg. "Hop round, girl, and see what you can find."

Meg fumbled in the darkness inside the door, finding a heap of letters on the floor. It was quite a handful she handed to Mrs Jarvis. Mrs Jarvis went through them slowly, murmuring "Pity! Pity! What a waste! Such nice envelopes. A pity you had to write my name on them." Then she turned briskly to the milkman.

"Well, Mr Duffy, I'm afraid I'm busy this morning. I'm only sorry your visit was all for nothing. Good morning," and she went back indoors again.

"She's a slippery customer, and no mistake," said Mr Duffy. "I'd like to see the old witch end up in gaol."

"But she's not a witch," said Meg.

"Well, what I'd call a witch, any road."

"She's too kind to be a witch," said Meg. "She really is. She saved my little brother when he might have been drowned. And she looked after me when I'd been searching for him all day. She's terribly kind, in spite of her funny ways."

"It's easy to be mistook," said Mr Duffy. "I've been caught too many times by her sort."

"She just doesn't think about money," said Meg, ready to make any excuses for her.

"Very convenient," said Mr Duffy.

"She's an artist, you see," said Meg.

"Artist, is she? Well, artist or witch, I don't see there's much to choose between 'em when it comes to money."

Mr Duffy was making a move towards the road.

"You're coming?" he asked.

"No," said Meg.

"You seem to mean it," he said. "She really was good to you, like you say? She helped you when you was needing help. You was in real trouble, was you?"

Meg assured him that they had been, and at last he seemed to believe her.

Maxie had come out of the house and was tugging at her sleeve. "I don't want to go," he said, "not until she's finished my picture."

As Meg walked with Mr Duffy up the private road, she told him all about Mrs Jarvis; how she had made up beds for them, and cooked for them, and how they ate fried bread with jam, and drank evaporated milk.

"D'you think she'd be offended," asked Mr Duffy, "if I left her a couple o' pints?"

They reached his van.

"Well," he said, "you say your mum and dad'll be back after tea. I reckon you'll be in good enough hands till then."

He drove off, and Meg carried the two pints back to Mrs Jarvis.

"Offended?" said Mrs Jarvis. "I'm shattered. He shames me. And now I'll just have to find the money somewhere. It's been nagging at me for ages."

Meg had been turning an idea over in her mind. She and Maxie had eaten most of Mrs Jarvis's food while they had been there. As far as she could see, there was nothing much left on the scullery shelves. But that veal and ham pie was still in the fridge at the cottage. She would fetch it back for lunch as a surprise. Then there were Maxie's shoes.

"I think I'll go home," she told Mrs Jarvis, "and fetch Maxie some shoes. It'd be a long way for him to walk back with bare feet."

"Good girl," said Mrs Jarvis. "I would never have thought of that."

Pleased with Mrs Jarvis's approval, and her own good idea, Meg set off up the track. It looked quite different by daylight. How strange never to be half scared of the private road again! Birds flew up out of the hedge as she passed, and once a baby rabbit scuttled across her path. From the corner by the finger post, she realized for the first time what a wonderful view there was through the gap in the opposite hedge, stretching across the fields away over to the village. Perhaps this was why Mrs Jarvis had so often been standing there, staring . . .

How nice she had been, and how kind! What a good thing Meg had thought of that pie! She skipped round the corner and out into the coast road. She would fetch Pokey too. Maxie would be pleased to see him again. She thought of Mrs Jarvis's sister, and tried to imagine if it had been Maxie in America, and her not having seen him for ten whole years, and not even being sure where he was. Surely that could never happen to them.

Or could it? How did you ever know what was going to happen.

She walked on, slower now, heading in the direction of the cottage. It seemed an unusually long way this morning. In spite of a good night's sleep she felt limp. She supposed she must still be tired after yesterday, though she had not noticed it at Mrs Jarvis's. Now she felt low, flat, and her head was beginning to ache. How much nicer if she could have been Maxie, sitting there in Rook Hall with Mrs Jarvis painting him, and giving him raisins, and calling him boy-o just as if he'd lived there for years.

And he had only been there one day. How long ago it seemed since yesterday morning! Was Hannah even now at the wedding? And what had happened to Granny Bennett? Was her mother really coming back after tea? Oh, she hoped so . . . Again 'it' wandered around in her thoughts, making her feel vaguely uneasy, apprehensive. Might they have gone to London partly about this thing they weren't yet ready to tell about? Perhaps to arrange about moving house, or going away . . .

At least the cottage was still there. She felt, as she turned in at the gate, as if she had surprised it in a little holiday of its own. Two blackbirds were feeding their young on the doorstep, seeming to know there was no danger of anyone opening the door behind them, and a spider's web was strung across the porch, looking as if it had been there for days. There was a dreaming look about the cottage; sleepy and sunlit, it might have been empty for weeks.

This must be how it looks when we aren't here, she thought, and found herself tiptoeing up the path as if she had no right there. The blackbirds flew up with cries of alarm. To give them time, she went over to the hedge and retrieved Maxie's doll from the long grass. It looked so harmless—pink, plastic, and altogether nondescript—that she could hardly believe it had seemed so frightening last night. And Maxie had thought she would like it! She untied it from its branch and carried it indoors.

Inside, too, the cottage looked different; so much smaller, so much lighter, so much tidier than she remembered. And so empty! She had never known it empty before—except last night, and then she had been in a panic. Now, compared with Rook Hall, it seemed light, white, and hollow, like a little box. The only thing out of place, apart from Pokey lying forlorn in his shoe on the kitchen table, was her mother's cardigan, thrown over the arm of a chair in the little sitting room. She picked it up and held it to her cheek, comforted by the familiar smell of safety.

But her head still ached. She wondered what her mother would have done. Told her to lie down, probably, and given her an aspirin. In a minute she would go and see if she could find one.

But first she must collect the things she had come for. Maxie's shoes. The veal and ham pie from the fridge; it would be more than enough for the three of them. Then there was that large jar of plums in the pantry, they would do for pudding. But what about all the milk? It made her head ache even more wondering what to do with all the milk. There were three pints in the fridge, and the milkman had left four more outside the back door.

She decided on three. They would take the cream off them to go with the plums. She left them on the kitchen table along with the other things. And Maxie's kite— he'd been wishing he had it with him to show to Mrs Jarvis. He'd be pleased at her remembering.

Then she went upstairs to look for the aspirin.

There were none in the bathroom. She went into her parents' bedroom and looked along the mantelpiece and on the chest of drawers. None there either. In the dressing table drawer perhaps . . . There were handkerchiefs, belts, a scarf, a tube of handcream, and a letter from Granny (her other granny, not Granny Bennett), but no aspirins. The letter was out of its envelope, lying on top of the folded handkerchiefs. She recognized the large clear handwriting immediately. It always accompanied her nicest birthday cards, her most imaginative presents. Sometimes, when she was younger, there had been little notes specially for her, enclosed in her mother's letters, in that same writing but larger, clearer.

This one was not for her, she knew, but it did start with 'Darling,' the way her own letters from Granny did. And the first words looked exciting. So she read on:

> *Darling, What lovely news! I wonder which 'It' will be, though it hardly matters now, having one of each already! Let me know what colour you'd like and I'll start knitting again. I'm sure you're right about getting a larger place. You could hardly cope with another where you are, but it'll be an awkward time to think of moving, surely? Or do you mean you plan to move at Easter when Mike will be on holiday? If only I had a larger flat! I might have taken one of them.*
>
> *I'm so glad you plan to tell Meg as soon as you're sure. I can't help feeling she was more upset than we realized when Maxie was born, having to be sent away like that, though I know there was no alternative at the time, and then coming back to find him installed. But of course she was too little to have it all explained then. My guess is she'll be thrilled about this one! and probably a great help to you.*

Slowly it dawned on Meg what she was reading. 'It'

was a baby! Her mother was going to have another baby. She felt dizzy with excitement—and relief. So the 'it' she had been worrying about all these weeks was nothing at all. At least, it was. It was a baby. She longed to tell someone—now—but there was no one to tell.

She put the letter back and ran downstairs again. Her hands were shaking with excitement as she packed the things in a basket. But her headache had miraculously cleared. No need for aspirin now. Only to get back quickly. She seized the basket, took a quick look round, and picked up the kite. She would have to carry that in her hand.

Off she went, the bottles of milk jostling each other in the basket to the accompaniment of her excited thoughts. A baby! Clink! A new baby! Clink! Clink! Clink! all the way down the track.

She imagined herself breaking the news. Guess what! We're going to have a new baby! It's already begun, but nobody knows yet—then she stopped, suddenly remembering that she herself was not supposed to know yet. So it was not her secret to tell. It was going to be like when she'd had her first dolls' pram—years ago—and found it in the bottom of her parents' wardrobe and played with it secretly, long before it had appeared on Christmas Day all wrapped up in holly paper. Only this was better—a grown up secret. It was the first grown up secret she had ever had a share in. No, she didn't want to tell it after all! Clink, clank, clank.

She skipped along so happily that the veal and ham pie jumped out of the top of the basket and rolled on to the grass verge. Luckily it had a paper wrapping. Then the kite slipped out from under her arm. She rearranged everything and set off at a more sober pace.

What had Granny meant about her being upset when Maxie was born? She had no memory of it—only of being taken into a strange room (which on second thoughts might have been her parents' bedroom) with her hat and coat on, and being shown a tiny red-faced baby. And everyone laughing because—as she'd been told later—she had said "Is it a monkey?" She remembered nothing of how she had felt—only a solemn, blank sort of feeling, and not wanting to leave go of her granny's hand. She was sure she had not made a scene or cried or anything. (Someone had given her a baby doll, she remembered. She'd never liked it and had bashed it up in a tantrum. But that had been later.) So why 'upset?' Certainly she was not upset now!

12

Goodbye to Mrs Jarvis

"You look as if you've had a whale of a time," said Mrs Jarvis in a surprised voice, as Meg dumped the loaded basket down on the table. "Whatever's all this? Surely your parents aren't back already?"

No, said Meg, smiling as she unpacked the things, but she had enjoyed herself just the same. And when Mrs Jarvis saw the pie, and the bottles of milk and the plums, she thought she knew the reason.

"Bless you, child! You're an angel to produce such a surprise," she said. "I thought we were going to have to eat nettles and search for birds' eggs. Now we can have a feast." And she unearthed a tin of baked beans from the back of the scullery cupboard, and found a forgotten bar of chocolate on one of the bookshelves. "Since we're having a feast, we may as well round it off properly," she said, and divided the chocolate into three.

"There's two little packets of nuts on the top shelf up there," said Maxie, pointing to the sideboard. "I saw them this morning."

"And there's a packet of crisps in that big jug on the

table," said Meg. "And another behind the type-writer."

"And here's a packet of biscuits," said Mrs Jarvis, looking in one of the saucepans. "Good, let's have them all out. I always forget what's where." She explained that she often left odd things like that around the place, then if she had forgotten to go shopping and suddenly found herself hungry, she would not starve.

"It makes mealtimes into a sort of treasure hunt sometimes," she said. "But disappointing when you don't find anything." She must remember to go shopping again this afternoon. In fact, she decided, she would go with Meg and Maxie when they left, before she forgot. This time she would be going to the little general shop at Nettleton. It was further to go, but the old man there was friendly. She would go in the boat as far as Nettleton marsh, so if Meg and Maxie would like a row with her first, she could then land them at the staithe and they could walk home.

So, lunch over, they set off together, walking across the fields behind Rook Hall—fields full of ragged robin and birds' eye, and scarlet poppies blowing in the wind—down to the edge of the creek. Here Mrs Jarvis's dinghy was pulled up on the bank below the dyke.

As they helped her pull it down to the water, Meg noticed a name painted on the stern in faded letters: *Sea Witch*. So that was why Mrs Pacey had called her the 'Sea witch woman!' But the boat had been named by whoever had owned it before. Mrs Jarvis had said she'd bought it as it was. And you could see it hadn't been painted for donkeys' years. How unfair of Mrs Pacey!

"In you get," said Mrs Jarvis. "She does leak a bit, but don't worry, you won't drown."

They got in, Mrs Jarvis gave the boat a final push off, picked up her long, raggedy skirt, and leapt in herself. She rowed like a man, pulling strongly against the tide which was now running out. They watched in admiration.

"You row better than Daddy," Maxie said.

"So I should. I row all the year round, not just on holidays."

But why had they never seen her, they asked? Because she chose to go out when no one was about, she said; sometimes early in the morning, when she went beachcombing if the tide was right. Sometimes in the evening, like yesterday, when other people had gone home. It all depended on the tides.

Beachcombing was fun, she said. She had found quite a few interesting things washed up by the tide. Had they noticed her carved lady, and her ship's bell? They had been particularly good finds. Once she had dragged home a huge lump of tallow, hoping to be able to make her own candles. She had had all her saucepans full of the stuff, melting it down. But it hadn't worked—something to do with the wicks. She'd used ordinary string, and they wouldn't stay alight. She got all her wood off the beach too. She never had to bother with coal in the winter time.

Not until they had been helped out of the boat and were standing on the shore, did it dawn on Meg and Maxie that the time had come to say goodbye to Mrs Jarvis. But they would be walking home by the road now, and she would be going on to Nettleton.

"I expect your mother will be back soon," she said.

"We didn't finish lunch till most people's teatime, so you'd better hurry along. When I've finished my shopping I shall drift home on the tide. So it's goodbye now." And before they had time to reply she had jumped back into the boat and was rowing away up the creek.

They stared after her. All the while in the boat, Meg had been listening to Mrs Jarvis, but at the same time the thought of the new baby had been dancing around in the back of her mind. Now she realized she had not even thanked her for having them.

"You didn't say goodbye properly," said Maxie in a reproachful voice.

"Nor did you. We didn't say thank you either." But that would make a good reason, she thought, for going to see Mrs Jarvis again.

Maxie was quiet on the way home, and Meg was glad. She was happy with her own thoughts. The sun slanted low over the fields, lighting up the yellow corn and the distant poplars. White seagulls flew slowly home from the fields to their sleeping place on the marsh. Suddenly Maxie let out a wail of disappointment. He had forgotten to bring his kite. He had left it at Rook Hall.

"Never mind," said Meg. "We can fetch it tomorrow. Anyway, Mummy'll be home soon. It doesn't matter now, does it?"

"No." His voice sounded small and resigned.

She glanced down at him. He was flagging a little. They had walked a long way these last two days. She felt a sudden pang of pity for him—to mind so much about a kite he hadn't even managed to fly properly yet! It seemed so unimportant compared with the thought of a new baby. Poor Maxie, he was neither big nor little, just a sort of spiky in-between.

It struck her for the first time that 'it', which would be so much more than all right for her, might not be all right for Maxie at all. She had always, secretly, longed for a new baby, but to Maxie it might feel as if he was losing something. She would still be the oldest, but he would be only the middle one; no longer the baby who everyone made a fuss of. Would he be able to bear it when people made more fuss of the new baby than of him? She remembered once hearing Nanny T say she had "always liked them little." I must tell her, she thought. Oh, poor Maxie.

They came to a field of cows. They none of them moved, except to give an occasional flick of their tails. Maxie had dropped behind. She turned and held out her hand. He gave a forlorn little skip and caught her up.

Passing the corner of the private road at last, they both looked hopefully to see if Mrs Jarvis might be coming up her little lane. But there was no sign of her.

"I expect she's still busy with the boat," said Meg, "pulling it up on the bank again. But we'll go again tomorrow, if they'll let us, and fetch your kite. That'll be nice, won't it?" Maxie nodded silently.

They went on up the road. Maxie had slipped her hand, and it was only a little way before he had dropped behind again. By the oak tree at the corner of their own lane, she waited for him.

"Have you got a pain?"

He put his hand to his forehead. "A heggeg, not a stummy cake."

That was all right. A headache, she knew, was sometimes his way of saying he felt sad.

"Never mind," she said, "they'll be home soon. Cheer up."

Again he nodded.

They turned into the lane. The car was at the gate, and Mr Bennett's back view was just disappearing into the cottage. They were back already!

Meg began to run, then saw that Maxie had stopped altogether. She realized suddenly why. It was nothing to do with the kite. She turned back to him.

"It doesn't matter about the frog," she said. "You needn't tell. And I won't either. You didn't really mean to, and he's all right now."

I didn't really mean to either, she thought, looking down at his anxious, crumpled little face. And because in that minute she felt she truly loved him—perhaps for the first time in her life—she gave him a rough little shove and said: "Abominable creature. Go on, I'll race you there!" And they dashed up the lane together.

Mr Bennett was already halfway up the stairs with the suitcase. He shouted down to them:

"Oh, there you are! I thought the place was a bit quiet. Down in a minute!"

Mrs Bennett came to the kitchen door, smiling. She looked tired but happy. They ran to her.

"Well, darlings, have you been good? You'll be glad to hear Granny Bennett's much better, isn't that nice? It was only a touch of 'flu. I took her a little pot plant from the two of you and she sent her love."

She put down her bags and parcels on the table, and looked at Meg with a sudden smile in her eyes.

"There are all sorts of things to tell you later—new pyjamas too. I got pale yellow with little flowers on, all right? But first let's get ourselves sorted out. Tea, I think." She filled the kettle and brought out the teapot, glancing brightly from one to the other of them.

"Nothing much has happened here, I suppose? We've only been away such a little time, haven't we? By the way, where's Hannah?"